Some Nightmares Are Real

Some Nightmares Are Real

The Haunting Truth Behind Alabama's Supernatural Tales

Kelly Kazek

Illustrated by **Sarah Cotton**

The University of Alabama Press

Tuscaloosa

The University of Alabama Press
Tuscaloosa, Alabama 35487-0380
uapress.ua.edu

Inquiries about reproducing material from this work should
be addressed to the University of Alabama Press.

Typeface: Source Serif

Cover image: *Old Mill Witch* by Sarah Cotton
Cover design: Lori Lynch

Cataloging-in-Publication data is available from the Library of Congress.
ISBN: 978-0-8173-2200-7
E-ISBN: 978-0-8173-9518-6

This book is dedicated to the memory of Kathryn Tucker Windham (1918–2011), a beloved Alabama storyteller and author who inspired many children to read, enjoy, and write ghost stories and to explore local legends. I first read her book *Thirteen Georgia Ghosts and Jeffrey* in 1974 at my elementary school in Warner Robins, Georgia; then, after moving to Alabama, I read her *Thirteen Alabama Ghosts and Jeffrey*. In the 2000s, when I was a newspaper editor, I met Ms. Windham when she spoke at the Alabama Press Association awards banquet. I was so impressed to learn about her pioneering role as a female journalist in the 1940s. I immediately bought her memoir *Odd Egg Editor* and learned more about her groundbreaking work. She was inducted into the Alabama Women's Hall of Fame in 2015 and the Alabama Writers Hall of Fame in 2023. Thank you, Ms. Windham, for inspiring little girls like me.

Contents

Introduction

A Love for Campfire Tales, Folklore, and Ghost Stories

An incident from my childhood is etched in my memory in detail as vivid and jumpy as an 8 mm film. It was summer, dark, and the Georgia woods were filled with the sounds of bullfrogs and cicadas. In my mind, like watching a reel from a 1970s vacation to Jekyll Island, I can see my six-year-old self running up the concrete patio steps from our backyard and banging my tiny fists on the sliding glass doors for my mother to let me in. I was wailing. I was terrified.

Earlier that night, my family (Mom, Dad, my older brother, and I) were joined by members of three other families for a barbecue in the backyard. By nightfall, we were sitting around a firepit near the edge of the woods behind our house. The fathers had decided to tell ghost stories. My mom and several others had gone inside to finish clearing the mess from the picnic tables.

I was one of the younger children there, with the oldest being thirteen. One dad—I forget which—began recounting the tale of Rawhead and Bloody Bones. The details of the legend are sketchy in my mind, probably because they were overridden by

1

the terror I felt in the dark of the woods that night. Suffice it to say, the title alone was enough to instill a thudding fear in my young heart and send me rushing from my log seat to the safety of the house.

Since then, I have researched the legend to try to recall details of the story. Most of the people who were there that night, including my parents, have died; others, like me, were too young to remember specifics. My research tells me that portions of the legend of "Rawhead and Bloody Bones" date to the 1600s in England. In the Southern United States, the names refer to two creatures who are part of one monster: "Rawhead" is a skull that bites its victims, and "Bloody Bones" is the creepy, dancing remains of his skeleton. In one version, "Rawhead" bites off the head of a person who was spreading gossip, a cautionary tale to those who might circulate unsubstantiated rumors.

In the half-century since that night, I have been fascinated with legends and folklore. At some point, my terror turned to curiosity. I can now enjoy a good, spooky story around a campfire without fear—although I still feel a creeping sensation on my back, as if eyes in the forest are watching. But what I love even more than a good story is a good story based on factual events.

I've never enjoyed those ghost-hunting shows in which teams wear night-vision goggles or bring equipment to record ghostly voices. My interest is in the tale itself, not in the "proving" or "disproving" of it. During my decades as a journalist, I was drawn to outsider art, roadside attractions, quirky history, and ghostly legends. When I wasn't reporting news stories, I was seeking out the weird and whimsical. Eventually, I stopped writing hard news altogether and became what I call a "weird news reporter," seeking out the "world's largest" objects (such as the world's largest Rubik's Cube, in Knoxville, Tennessee, or the world's largest catsup bottle, in Collinsville, Illinois), or people who create art from found objects, or "hauntings" based on an area's very real history.

In this book, I wanted to share folklore in the form of ghost stories from Alabama, my home state since I was twelve years old (when I moved to Huntsville from Georgia). In high school, my friends and I enacted all the rituals of teenhood in the 1980s—driving over supposedly haunted bridges, scaring ourselves in cemeteries or searching for ghosts (including the spirits that supposedly haunted the Dead Children's Playground, which is described in this book).

That's what folklore is: orally passing down a community's stories or beliefs. Of course, the stories change with the tellings. That is part of the fascination of folklore. But the stories are grounded in truth, in historical places, people, and times. The lore that follows is all based on real places and people in Alabama. I have framed the stories with invented tales, told in the manner in which they might be recounted around a campfire, and created fictional characters who thrill to the folklore in the same way that my friends and I did as kids. A section in the back of this book tells readers which parts of the stories are real and provides information on places related to the stories that they can actually visit.

I tried to avoid legends that had been widely recounted in other books, including Kathryn Tucker Windham's beloved Thirteen Ghosts and Jeffrey series. The point of folklore, however, is that it is repeated through generations. In today's world, that means stories that have likely been recorded somewhere on the vast internet, so elements of all of the stories can likely be found online.

Introduction

There are those who believe telling ghost tales is somehow evil or anti-religious. I believe it has a different purpose: folklore, in many cases, was a way to explain phenomena that was then considered unexplainable—thus the use of supernatural elements—or to provide lessons to frighten people into doing what was considered "right," or "safe" (such as not walking alone at night on isolated roads).

I hope you will enjoy these tales for what they are: a tribute to the time-honored process of passing lore from one person to another. Once I have told you these stories, you can keep them going by telling them yourself! Perhaps you can visit some of the real places mentioned in this book and learn some history of the great state of Alabama. Most important, I hope you get just scared enough to pull the covers up to your chin. Don't forget to leave the bedside light on.

LEGEND 1

The People Under the Lake

"People used to live down there, you know. Under the lake," Jake said, looking over the side of the johnboat into the dark water of Weiss Lake. Ricky, who was often one step behind Jake mimicking his every action in adoration of the older boy, followed his gaze but saw only his own reflection on the surface. It was impossible to see anything beneath the water; its normal deep blue took on an almost purplish hue at its deepest. But Jake continued to try to peer into the depths of the impenetrable surface. "I've heard some people are still down there."

Ricky's reflected eyes grew big.

"Jake McClellan!" Maggie Bartlett scolded her friend, rolling her eyes. "Stop trying to scare Ricky." Maggie's little brother was only twelve and their parents had forced her to bring him along. She knew her little brother served as a sort of chaperone. She and Jake weren't allowed to take his folks' fancy ski boat out alone, not until next year when they would be seniors in high school. Instead, they'd brought the smaller boat Mr. McClellan used for bass fishing.

"I'm not kidding," Jake insisted, changing direction to angle the boat toward the shore of a small island where they planned to pull out the cooler and have some drinks and late afternoon snacks on the strip of sand. The three had spent most of the day on Weiss Lake and the sun had made the Bartlett siblings' skin glow a deep pink—but not Jake's. He lived with his folks in a house on the lake and he was on the water anytime his parents let him. His skin was a deep golden-brown color that reminded Maggie of Grammy's pecan pie.

"People really did live down there before the 1950s," Jake continued. "There were farms and churches and cemeteries and all kinds of things that now sit on the bottom, fifty, sixty feet beneath our boat. There are people still down there . . . or at least their bodies."

Ricky shivered and Maggie gave Jake a warning look.

"*Bodies?*" Ricky squeaked. "Are there really *bodies* down there?" As Jake neared the island, he stopped the motor and hopped out of the boat into the shallow water so he could pull the small craft to the sandy beach. When the boat dragged on the sandy bottom, he motioned for the others to hop out. Maggie stepped into the water and noticed Ricky had paused to look into the water, which now only came up as high as his knees.

Jake neatly pulled the empty boat far enough onto the sand to secure it. "Yes, bodies. They didn't always move the bodies in the cemeteries before they flooded the land, before they made the lake."

"What do you mean before 'they made' the lake? Doesn't nature kinda make the lakes?" Ricky looked up from the water, pushing his glasses back on his sun-reddened nose. It was probably going to peel, along with the sliver of his shoulder not covered by the life jacket, Maggie thought. Her mother would blame her for not making her brother put on sunscreen.

"No, Squirt," Jake said, pulling the bulky cooler from the bottom of the boat. "Lots of lakes are man-made. In Alabama, all of the big lakes are artificial. People would just decide they needed lakes in certain areas and then dam the water and control the flow to create power. It's all about the *simoleons*," Jake said, rubbing his fingers together as if holding money. "Haven't you taken social studies class?" Ricky shook his head. Alabama history was taught to all fourth-grade classes in public schools, but Ricky had not learned about the lakes in his class two years before.

Suddenly, Ricky let out a shriek and splashed the last few feet toward the beach.

"What is it?" Maggie said with a squawk of her own, automatically moving inland, just in case he had encountered some sort of underwater creepy-crawly. Ricky limped to a large fallen log next to an old firepit, left by countless teens before them. He shook his head. "I don't know," he said. "All of a sudden, the ground seemed to give way beneath my foot, and it twisted a little. For a minute, it felt like I was being sucked down."

"Sit down and let me look," Maggie demanded in the motherly tone she used with Ricky whenever Mom wasn't around. The ankle was slightly red but otherwise unblemished. "Looks okay to me," she said. "Maybe you just stepped in a hole."

Jake's grin looked a little too self-satisfied for Maggie's taste. That typically meant he was up to one of his pranks. She loved him but he sure could be exasperating. "Jake," she said in a warning tone. "What did you do?"

"Me? I didn't *do* anything," he said. "I just know what it was he stepped in."

7

Maggie's and Ricky's heads turned toward Jake at the same time and angle, like a couple of meerkats who spotted food. "You do?" Ricky asked.

Jake nodded. "It was a grave," he said, lowering his voice ominously.

"Stop it, Jake!" Maggie commanded. She hated when he tried to scare Ricky.

"I'm telling the truth," he said. "And I can prove it. Come stand right here."

Jake stood with his toes touching the lapping lake and pointed straight ahead with Ricky and Maggie standing cautiously behind him. "See how low the water is here? And how we could just walk the boat onto the beach? That's because we've been in a drought for two months and the water is low. It's the only time you can really see them."

"I don't see anything," Ricky said.

"Come over here where the sun isn't hitting the water." It was shallow enough that the kids could have walked twenty or thirty feet without even getting their knees wet. The lake water was nice and clear in this shallow pool. Jake pointed. "See right there?"

"I only see some dark spots in the dirt under the water," Ricky said with a shrug.

"Yeah, and what shape are they?" Jake asked.

Ricky looked more closely. "Rectangles," he said. "I see dark rectangles in the sand beneath the water." Ricky looked to Jake for confirmation.

"Yep. And what kinds of things are rectangular?"

Ricky looked back and noticed the rectangles were all human-sized and were perfectly lined up beneath the clear water.

"Graves," Maggie said in a heavy voice. "Graves. You just had us walking through graves." She punched Jake in the arm as her annoyance rose. "What if what Ricky stepped on was someone's body?"

Ricky shuddered.

Jake shrugged. "The official story is there are no bodies here . . . but that's not what I think," he said. "This used to be Lawrence Cemetery and the power company claims it moved the bodies before flooding the area in the 1960s."

Ricky pushed his glasses back on his nose. "So you weren't making that up before? About flooding towns to build power dams?"

"Nope," Jake said. "That's why I brought you here. You can only see these when there's a pretty severe drought and the lake levels are much lower than normal. Want to hear the story?"

The sun had begun its slow descent. Maggie was feeling a bit creeped out herself, but Ricky nodded vigorously, caught in the spell of Jake's tale.

"We really should go so we can get back across the lake before dark," Maggie said. She glanced nervously at the lowering sun.

"We have plenty of time," Jake said, glancing up. "The story is not very long. If y'all sit down and listen, we'll head straight back to my house afterward."

"Yeah, c'mon, Mags," Ricky said excitedly. "I want to hear." He turned to Jake. "How do you know so much anyway?"

Jake smiled. "I've lived on this lake my whole life," he said. "I hear stuff. Plus, I did my sophomore project on how all the major lakes in Alabama were made, including this one. I called it 'Drowned Towns.' Only *A* I ever earned."

"Okay," Maggie said, grudgingly. She wouldn't admit it, but now she was interested too. "But make it quick, okay?"

9

Jake pulled a bottle of Sun Drop from the cooler, cozied up to the long-dead coals from previous fires, and said, "just settle around the firepit, grab a Coke, and listen . . . "

Some of the old-timers say, on quiet nights, boaters have heard the ghostly chimes of church bells rising from beneath Weiss Lake. Sometimes, the eerie baying of unseen coonhounds will echo across the water, said to be the spirits of hunting dogs whose graves were never moved before the dam was built and the farmlands flooded. Still others have reported seeing ghostly figures appearing atop the water, hovering, trying to find their homes. At least, that's what legends say . . .

Lots of small communities were submerged beneath Alabama's man-made lakes from the 1910s through the 1960s by the state's big power companies, Alabama Power Company and the Tennessee Valley Authority. Building dams not only created electricity in rural areas and jobs in the wake of the Great Depression and World War II, the projects also created recreational areas, where people could boat and fish and water-ski. The waterways brought tourists to the state.

"So, these big companies say they moved the towns before they were flooded and, mostly, they did—bought the houses and churches and schools and tore them down," Jake explained. "I mean, it makes sense, right? They couldn't leave a church with a steeple so high it would catch the bottom of a boat. They wouldn't leave a valuable house just for fish to swim through." He continued his story.

To create all those lakes in Alabama the power companies had to move thousands of people—living and dead—to land outside the flood zones. First, dams were built in nearby rivers, then engineers surveyed and determined what the pool level was going to be, and which homes would be impacted by the reservoir. Then power company representatives headed out with their checkbooks, offering people—usually—a fair market price for homes and land.

"On some farms, smaller outbuildings, like small barns and sheds, were left behind," Jake said. "What was surprising was how many big old homes, mansions even, were left beneath the lake. Some of the well-off folks paid to have their nice homes hooked up to trailers and moved to higher land. I saw an old black-and-white photo of a big old mansion called Snow Hill being moved along a dirt road to higher ground. But lots were torn down—and some were nearly one hundred years old."

"So, what about the dead people?" Ricky pressed for a definitive answer, wanting to know—and not wanting to—if he'd actually stepped in a grave. He pointed to the rectangles, their shadows deepening beneath the shallow surface as the sun lowered. "Are there still some under here?"

Jake shrugged. "Depends on who you believe. When I was researching my project, I found actual cemetery relocation forms used by some power companies when they were creating the lakes. They went to surviving family members and offered to move the bodies to cemeteries that would be above water so their folks could still visit them. They would just dig them up and move the caskets and the headstones to another graveyard. The problem was, some of the graves had been there since the 1800s and there were no family members around anymore.

There was no one to visit the graves so . . . no reason to move the bodies. No one really knows what happened to those remains, but most locals think the bodies are still down there."

The kids were hushed, except for the sound of Jake crunching on some Doritos, while they thought about the bodies potentially buried a few feet away.

"That's creepy," Ricky said, trying to keep the tremor from his voice. He grabbed the Doritos from Jake and chewed nervously and noisily.

"What's creepy is what some of the old folks told me for my project. I went over to Valley View nursing home like my teacher suggested and talked to some people there. Old Mr. Hooie—remember him; he used to own the bait shop?—he told me one of the creepiest tales I'd ever heard."

Ricky and Mags didn't speak, which Jake took as a green light to resume his storytelling. "He was out in his bass boat one night with Mrs. Hooie. It was getting dark, and Mrs. H. was pressing Mr. H. to get back to the house before it got too dark to see the dock. So Mr. H. tells me, he said . . ." Jake changed his voice to a deeper, more Southern tone to imitate Mr. Hooie and continued, "'The missus just kept jawin' and naggin' at me 'til I finally accused of her being a'scairt.' 'I *am* scairt!' she says. 'I've heard the stories just like you have, about the bodies under the lake that come out at night to walk on the water, the spirits of people looking for their lost homes.' Mr. H. told his wife that, of course, that was a lot of 'claptrap,' but he packed up his gear anyway and was about to start the motor to head to shore. That's when they heard it. The sound of church bells that seemed to rise up from under the lake and ripple in echoes outward, according to Mr. H."

"Mrs. Hooie looked terrified. 'See I told you,' she said, nervously. 'Let's get out of here!' Mr. H. pulled the engine cord, but it only sputtered. Before he could pull again, he looked at Mrs. Hooie and saw her eyes were as big around as cathead biscuits. He followed her gaze and saw the clear-but-shimmery form of a man in old-timey clothes—like a farmer's Sunday suit. The apparition walked on top of the surface of the lake, but it continued looking down, worried, with a hat in his hands, like he was trying to see something beneath the surface."

Jake continued in a dramatic fashion: "Mr. Hooie pulled the cord again and the motor sprang to life. He gave it a bit too much gas in his hurry to get out of there and it lurched forward. When he finally looked back the figure was gone. He told me Mrs. H. didn't say a word all the way home. She was never the same after that and she never would go on the lake again."

"Okay, that's enough," Mags said, standing and gathering their empties to stash in the cooler. By then, the sky had changed from pinks and oranges to a deepening purple. "I'm ready to go. *Now.*" She could tell by his face that Ricky was truly afraid, and she realized they were going to have to walk past the underwater graves again to get the boat off the beach.

Jake noticed her apprehension. "Don't worry," he said, realizing he may have pushed too far. "Y'all can hop in here on the beach and I can use the oars to push us until the water is deep enough to run the motor."

Mags's breath released in a *whoosh*. After they'd gathered their snacks and trash, she helped Ricky into the johnboat, then she climbed in herself. Jake walked the boat out, struggling a little with their added weight, until the water reached his knees, seemingly unconcerned about the dark rectangles in the dirt. Just as Jake was about to hop in and row to deeper water, he lurched, as if something had grabbed him. He tried jumping in the boat again but splashed back to the water.

"What is it? Get in! We need to leave," Mags said, her voice sounding urgent now.

"I'm trying," Jake said, sounding mystified. "Something is pulling my ankle."

"You stop joking right this minute and get in the boat!" Mags said in her most determined and stern mother's voice.

"I'm not joking . . . something has my left leg," Jake said. Now even he sounded frightened.

Finally, he managed to heave himself into the boat, pulling the left leg as hard as he could from the bottom of the lake. Maggie grabbed an oar to help row and they pushed through the water as fast as they could. After rowing for thirty or forty yards, they set down the oars and Jake prepared to start the small motor. Just as his hand reached the pull cord, they heard the deep clang of a bell ring out—but it sounded muffled, as if its clapper was wrapped in cotton.

"Hurry, Jake," Maggie cried.

"Yes, I want to go home," Ricky cried plaintively. Just before the sound of the bell faded, Ricky saw, in the fading light, the figure of a man wearing a suit and hat from the old days, like the 1920s or '30s. The figure seemed to walk on top of the water, looking down as if searching for something beneath the surface.

Ricky pointed a shaky finger and the others' gaze followed its direction.

"What the . . . ?" Jake said.

Maggie, who hadn't believed in ghosts that morning, shuddered. "Please hurry," she whispered as the figure of the man shimmered in front of them, starting to come apart like a cloud on a windy day—an arm floating away here and a leg fading away there. Finally, the figure was nothing but a mist. Jake gave another hard tug and the engine burped and sputtered

14

before settling into a smooth hum. The boat shot across the lake. When Jake looked back where the apparition had been, he saw nothing.

When they finally reached the McClellans' dock, Maggie was really worried about Ricky. He hadn't said a word since they saw the strange figure.

"Are you okay, Ricky?" He nodded but looked pale. "Please don't tell Mom and Dad. They'll never let us go anywhere with Jake again," Maggie pleaded.

Ricky merely stared back across the lake to where the figure had been. He didn't acknowledge his sister's plea. "Help me get him on the dock, would ya?" she asked Jake, pulling Ricky to his feet.

"Sure," Jake said, climbing out and tying off the boat. As he held his hands down to help pull Ricky to the dock, Mags saw Jake's ankle.

"Jake!" she cried. "What is that?" His ankle was red and swollen.

"It's nothing," he said, pulling Ricky onto the plank platform and shrugging aside Maggie's concerns. "It probably just got tangled in some water hyacinth."

"It wasn't water hyacinth," Ricky said in a small and wooden voice.

"What? How do you know?" Jake asked. Ricky pointed at his own ankle, the one that had sunk into the sand where the graves were located. Mags looked closely and could see a red mark encircling his ankle and small bruises the size of the pads of fingers, as if he had been grabbed by a hand. Maggie looked back at Jake's foot. There, she saw the same thing: Fingerprints around his ankle.

She shuddered. "C'mon, let's get inside," she said, hopping

out onto the dock. As she and Jake helped Ricky up the stairs toward the yard, Maggie glanced back at the water and thought she noticed something else. She hoped, she prayed, she was wrong. There, just beneath the surface, a human-shaped shadow moved down toward the murky depths.

LEGEND 2

The Dead Children's Playground

"**I** am not going in there at night," Becks said, shaking her strawberry blonde curls for emphasis. "I don't care what you say. Not only because of the ghosts but because the park is closed after dark, and I've heard the police drive by there all the time. I am not going to get into trouble for some silly ghost hunt."

"You're just scared," Max said with a laugh.

"Of course, she is," Rhonda responded. "Anyone who has ever heard of the Dead Children's Playground is scared of it. I mean, it's called '*dead children's playground*,' for Jiminy's sake. Just saying the words together gives me goosebumps. I'm with Becks on this one."

"What if we go during the day?" Clay said. Max made a face of disgust. Going during the daytime didn't require any real bravery.

The Dead Children's Playground was a very real park in Huntsville that just happened to adjoin one of the largest and oldest burial grounds in the state, Maple Hill Cemetery. The geography of the location only added to its aura of mystery—it was set in a natural alcove closed on three sides by rock walls so that the park was often in shadow, even on the brightest summer day. On that day, in early August, the weather was expected to be scorching, but Max and Clay were determined not to let their last few days of summer before their senior year go to waste.

Becks looked doubtful but Rhonda said, "C'mon, Becks. All kinds of parents and kids—*alive* ones—go there during the day. It'll be fine. We'll show the boys there's nothing there and be done with it. They *did* go shopping with us last week for new school clothes."

Becks considered a moment. "Fine," she said. "But I still think it's stupid."

Clay hollered "shotgun!" and raced to the car, but Becks put her hands on her hips and stood silently, letting him and Max know that *she* was riding in the front passenger seat. Max knew he couldn't afford to make his girlfriend any angrier with him. "C'mon, Clay, you know Becks is riding up front with me," he said.

Clay hopped in back beside Rhonda, whom he kinda sorta dated from time to time just because the four of them were always together. Really, Clay and Rhonda were more friends than love interests.

Max turned the radio up high and that, combined with the rush of the wind from the windows, meant there was no use trying to hold a conversation as they drove. Instead, Becks thought back to what she knew about the Dead Children's Playground. There was one story she knew better than the others, mainly because her mother had told it to her. It was the story of her great-grandmother Grace Swanner.

It was October 1918, and Grace's family had just gotten word her big brother Ellis would be coming home from the Great War in a military casket. The fighting was over, and he had survived the battles, but another enemy had arrived, and this enemy didn't choose allegiances—it killed nearly everyone in its path. It was the Spanish Influenza, or what the old folks sometimes called the *grippe*, and it was killing people in all parts of the world. Some people wondered if the epidemic was God's punishment for the horrible deeds carried out in a war that had affected the entire world.

Grace, who had just turned eleven, didn't know if the flu was God's retribution but she did know her world had changed overnight. The announcement came in the newspaper the day after her birthday on September 28—the Spanish flu had arrived in Huntsville. And now, only three weeks later, the once-bustling city of Huntsville was practically a ghost town.

By October 5, flu cases had topped 1,000 in Huntsville. The disease had a rapid onset, with people becoming extremely ill within a day of contact with an infected person and, in the worst cases, dying within three days.

On October 7, Alabama governor Charles Henderson had ordered all schools closed in an effort to stop the spread of the dreaded disease. All school and church activities, including the Boy Scouts' Halloween party and the cakewalk fundraiser, had been canceled. By October 13, all public offices had closed and two days later, Governor Henderson ordered the theaters, restaurants, salons, and stores—except groceries and pharmacies—to close. Not that Grace's mother needed an order from the governor: she had already forbidden Grace and her little brother, Hank, from going to visit friends or even walking to the corner store.

Then, on October 18, a telegram arrived; in just a few short words, it said that Private Ellis Anderson Swanner, survivor of trench warfare, had died of Spanish flu in a hospital in Brest, France. Grace's mother was devastated, and Grace's father had to get the doctor to prescribe pills to help her sleep. Mrs. Swanner took to her bed and stayed in the darkened room for three days. When she came out, she seemed to Grace to be just a faint copy of her once-vivacious self. She used to sing in the kitchen—"Rockabye Your Baby" or "Bill Bailey"—and grab up one of the children for a quick dance through the living room. Now, she never danced or sang. In fact, she rarely spoke.

No one ever said so, but Grace understood it was her job to occupy Hank and keep him from bothering their mother. It wasn't easy with school and the movie houses and even the playgrounds closed; Hank was a rambunctious eight-year-old, often running through the house with a cap gun, his penny-colored hair topped with a toy doughboy helmet. Grace also began cooking breakfast, since it took her mother longer to get out of bed in the mornings. First, Grace would get the newspaper from the porch and sneak looks at the obituaries before leaving the paper beside her father's plate. She was shocked sometimes to find the names of some of her friends listed there. She asked her father once if she could go to the funeral of her classmate Agnes Teague. They weren't best friends, but she was part of a group of girls that had played together at recess. Her father shook his head sadly. "They aren't holding funerals now," he said. "People who were contagious are buried just as fast as someone can dig the grave." He saw the horrified expression on Grace's young face. "A funeral's no place for a little girl, anyway."

But Grace didn't feel like a little girl anymore. Mostly, she just felt scared. Father still went to his law office some days and he would stop at the store once a week for flour and bread and fruit. The milk and eggs were delivered to their porch every week, but Father insisted that Grace clean each milk bottle and each egg with soap and a cloth before putting them away. The only time Grace and Hank were allowed out was to walk to the end of the street and back, as long as they wore their face masks to prevent catching airborne germs and didn't play with any of the other children. Sometimes, on their walks, Grace would see her best friend, Lorna, looking from the window of her upstairs bedroom. The friends waved wistfully to one another.

When they passed their elementary school, dark and quiet without the throngs of children, Grace read the urgent signs taped to the windows of the front doors:

WEAR a MASK and SAVE YOUR LIFE!!

and

Spitting spreads Spanish Flu!
DON'T SPIT!

Another from the US Public Health Office said:

INFLUENZA
Spread by Droplets sprayed from Nose and Throat

Cover each COUGH and SNEEZE with handkerchief
Spread by contact.
AVOID CROWDS.
If possible, WALK TO WORK.

Do not spit on floor or sidewalk.
Do not use common drinking cups and common
towels.
Avoid excessive fatigue
If taken ill, go to bed and send for a doctor.

Once, Grace noticed a poem in lovely handwriting that indicated it was penned by a teacher. It was a verse she'd heard other girls recite while jumping rope before the school closed.

> I had a little bird,
> Its name was Enza.
> I opened the window,
> And in flew Enza.

Grace read it twice before realizing the last line referred to "influenza." She knew it was meant to be a warning to keep their windows closed so the germs could not get in (though this was, tragically, the exact opposite of what they should have been doing to stem the spread). Sometimes at night, she'd lie in bed imaging the invisible germs and tiny bugs crawling beneath the doors to their home, trying to get to the rest of her family.

Her nightmare came true one day when her father arrived home from town with a deep cough, a fever of 102.5°F, and a sign he'd picked up at the Red Cross office. Grace should tape it to the front door, he said, and leave it there until he was feeling better, which he was sure would be in no time.

It read, in large red letters:

QUARANTINE

"But, Father, we have to call the doctor," Grace said, her fear mounting. Mother was in the bedroom taking an afternoon nap, which had become her habit. She was always tired.

Mr. Swanner shook his head. "I already went to Doc Biffle's office on my way home," he said. "He's the only one still seeing patients even though he didn't seem well himself. The others are all sick or have died, even most of the druggists. . . ." Father trailed off as if realizing he'd said too much. He needed Grace to be strong right now and not paralyzed with fear.

As soon as the words were out of his mouth, Grace recalled reading the headline in the newspaper: "Huntsville Seeks Help after All Pharmacists and All but One Physician Stricken with Flu." Grace helped Father to bed, trying not to let fear engulf her. "Come on, Father, get into bed. I'll heat some soup." She suddenly stopped. "Wait," she said. "You can't get in with Mother. What if you give it to her, too?"

The look in Father's eyes told Gracie what she needed to know.

"I'm afraid it's too late, Gracie Bug," he said. "We've all been in close contact. Doc Biffle said we can't tell if you or Hank or Mother already have the bug so we can't risk exposing anyone else. That's why we have to put up the sign, so no one will come in. Anyway, there is no treatment, so we'll just have to pray. Pray hard."

Grace felt panic bloom in her stomach and fill her body. If she couldn't go out and no one could come in, what would she do? She wished Mother were her old self.

"Don't worry," Mr. Swanner said. "I arranged with Mr. Fuqua to deliver groceries every Tuesday morning. He'll just leave them under the carport."

Grace hid her terror and helped Father into bed.

Becks was the first one out of the car when the group reached Maple Hill Park. "Before we go to the park," she said. "I want to show y'all something."

The group followed her past the park entrance and into the cemetery. Becks looked down the rows of headstones as they walked along several paved, tree-lined lanes.

"C'mon, Becks," Max said, wiping sweat from his brow. "It's hot, even in the shade. What are you looking for?"

She suddenly pointed. "There it is!" She walked among the headstones until she reached a simple wide granite stone etched SWANNER.

"Looks like an entire family," Clay said.

"Those are my relatives," she said. They looked at the names and dates.

James Earl 1875-1918

Edna Louise 1880-1918

Ellis Anderson 1899-1918

Henry Harmon 1910-1918

Near the large headstone was a smaller one that read:

Rebecca Grace Swanner Mendenhall 1907-1987

"Hey, they all died in 1918 except this one . . . Rebecca Grace," Max said.

"Yep," Becks said. "They all died in the flu pandemic. Grace nursed them and tried to save them, but she was only a little girl. After they died, she was raised by her aunt Margaret. Grace went on to have five kids of her own, including my granddad, Bud. I'm named for her."

The group was quiet for a bit, thinking of the family that was nearly wiped out by influenza. And the children were so young!

"There wasn't a headstone here for years. No one to pay for one," Becks continued. "Not until after Grace died. Before she died of cancer, she found records of where they were buried and left enough money in her will for the marker."

Max, still mopping sweat beads from his forehead, grew impatient.

"Let's go! It'll be cooler in the park, too."

When the group arrived at the park, it was late afternoon. It was still hot, but the sun was lower, and the air was cooler within the three stone walls of the park. Two young women were chatting on a bench, watching three children play. Far from creeping out kids and parents, the park was beloved in the community; in 2007 when the cemetery commission had tried to buy the property for an expansion, the outcry was large enough that the city ended up keeping it as a park. The parks and recreation board even installed new playground equipment, replacing the U-shaped swings on their rusty chains and the aging metal slide with a new swing set and a brightly colored plastic climbing apparatus.

The four teens went to the swing set and Rhonda hopped onto a seat. "Push me!" she demanded of Clay, who obliged. Becks sat in the swing beside her and Max also pushed her higher and higher until she laughed and squealed, "Let me off!" When the girls got off the swings, they noticed the women and children had gone and shadows were creeping over the play area. The playground that had just seemed like a kid's dream suddenly seemed cold and dark despite the August heat. Becks shuddered and wrapped her arms across her chest.

"You can't possibly be cold," Max said. "It's got to still be ninety-five degrees out here."

Becks laughed nervously. "I just . . . I just felt a little chill, that's all."

Rhonda had gone over to the climbing wall and clambered up the slide that was only about as high as she was tall. "Look!" she said suddenly, pointing to the swing set.

Two of the four swings were moving as if someone were sitting in them.

"They're just still moving from where we touched them, is all," Clay said.

"But . . . those aren't the swings we used," Becks said. "C'mon, Max. You've had your fun. Now let's go."

"Okay, fine," he said, "but you're being silly. It's just the wind. Or something."

The four turned to walk up the steps of the small incline to the parking lot with Becks bringing up the rear. She was lost in thought about her brave great-grandmother and the family she never knew. She had just stepped on the bottom step when she heard a sound. It was like a light giggle—a child's giggle. Becks turned quickly and saw the figure of a little girl, laughing as she ran across the playground. For just a moment—no more than a second—a streak of sun flashed through the trees at the top of the rock wall, and she thought she saw a glint of penny-colored hair. Then the apparition was gone.

"Becks?" Rhonda said from the top of the steps. "You coming?"

"Coming," she said and hurried to the car.

The Wolf Woman of Mobile

"Watch this," Dusty said, his voice traveling on the wake of air created by the speed of his banana-seat Huffy bicycle, the latest 1971 model he'd gotten for his birthday the month before. As the words floated back and into Mink's ears, she saw the front tire of Dusty's bike come off the ground as he popped a wheelie. Mink wasn't too impressed, but she took one hand off the handlebars of her own bike long enough to give him a thumbs up. Dusty always did like more than his share of praise.

They were headed to the Kwickie on the corner of their street to buy some Wacky Packages, collectible stickers spoofing popular products such as "Chimps Ahoy!" and "Crust Toothpaste." If the packs contained any stickers that weren't duplicates, they'd go to Mink's basement and sort and file them into the binders where they stored their collection. They used the duplicates to trade with Cleve and Bub-Eye, brothers who lived in the center of the cul-de-sac between the houses where Dusty and Mink lived. Sometimes Mink got tired of playing only with boys but, when school was out and she couldn't see Fern or

Missy, she was relegated to being the fourth to the boys' Three Musketeers. And now that it was the first week of April, there were only seven weeks left of sixth grade at their school, which was located two blocks from their modest subdivision in Mobile, Alabama.

Dusty and Mink tore into their packs, two each, the minute they left the store. Mink was annoyed to see yet another duplicate of the "Crust Toothpaste" sticker but perked up when she saw coveted "Skimpy" peanut butter and "Band-Ache" stickers, which she didn't have.

When they neared their cul-de-sac, Dusty slowed his Huffy until he and Mink were riding side by side. "Wonder what's going on?" he asked.

That's when Mink saw that Cleve and Bub-Eye were standing in the cul-de-sac with their mom and dad, as well as Mink's and Dusty's parents. They pedaled faster and, as they approached, they heard Mr. Wrangler, Cleve and Bub-Eye's dad, saying, "This is the last warning. You're going to go too far with your pranks one of these days."

"But Dad!" Cleve exclaimed. "We're not joking. We saw something, right there at the edge of the woods."

Bub-Eye, who was only in fifth grade, piped up: "It was a monster."

"Enough of that," Mrs. Wrangler said, pulling her cardigan closer in the dusky spring breeze. She turned to Pat Devereaux, Mink's mom, and Sueann Rutledge, Dusty's mom.

"I'm sorry if they frightened you." The grown-ups murmured that they weren't frightened and boys will be boys as they made their way to their respective front doors, laughing . . . but nervously, Mink thought.

Dusty and Mink stopped their bikes beside the Wrangler

boys, who were staring after the adults in confusion. "Why won't they believe us?" Bub-Eye said.

"Maybe because you lie all the time? Last week you tried telling your mom school was ending early this year so you wouldn't have to take that math test," Mink said, even though she had no idea what the current tale was.

Cleve ignored the barb. "But we really did see it," Cleve said in a pleading tone.

"What *did* you see?" Dusty asked.

"A monster. I saw a monster right over there by the fort." He pointed to the head of the trail that looked like a gaping doorway carved out of the brush by years of kids tramping through there to get to the fort they'd built in the woods.

Mink barked out a laugh. "A monster? Really, Cleve?"

"It's true," he replied.

He began to describe what he had seen: a hairy creature that walked on four legs like a dog but with facial features like a human.

"She had long flowy hair on her head and the rest of her body was covered in fur, like a wolf's. And at one point she stood on her hind legs, like a person. And those eyes . . ." he shuddered. "They were like black marbles."

Dusty snorted in disbelief, but Mink suddenly understood Cleve was telling the truth. He had seen *something*. And he was afraid. Plus, Bub-Eye looked like he was on the verge of tears.

Mink pictured an elegant-but-terrifying creature whose body looked and moved like a wolf's but whose face had a human-like nose, mouth, and eyes that gave the impression of sentience.

"It was probably just a dog," she said to be comforting.

"Maybe," Cleve said uncertainly, eyeing the trailhead in the tree line. "But I've never seen a dog like that. Or even a wolf like that. C'mon, Bub, it's time for dinner." Cleve and Bub-Eye almost never went inside before being forced by a series of incrementally more insistent calls from Mrs. Wrangler. Now, they seemed truly unnerved.

Rather than sorting their loot as planned, Dusty and Mink decided to return to their homes and try to eavesdrop on their parents to learn more about the Wolf Woman the Wrangler brothers had seen. "See ya tomorrow," Dusty called. Mink didn't respond. She continued to think about the long-haired creature that could stand on its hind legs and imagine those dark, glassy eyes.

Mink's parents talked of nothing at dinner except what plants Mrs. Devereaux was planning to buy at the Order of the Moose Women's Auxiliary plant sale the next weekend and where she was going to plant them.

As Mink readied for bed that night, her mother commented that Mink hadn't eaten much of the Hamburger Helper she'd made for dinner. Mink loved the new-fangled grocery item because it was like eating macaroni and hamburgers all mushed together; her mom loved it because it came in a single box and only took a few minutes to make. When Mink didn't eat her entire serving, her mother was worried. She felt Mink's head and determined she didn't have a fever.

"I'm just tired," Mink told her mother. Her mom tucked her in as if she were still a little kid, pulling the pink gingham bedspread up to her chin and kissing her forehead. "Night, Sugar Lump."

"Night, Mama," she said.

Mink pulled her Raggedy Ann from behind her pillow and mashed her face into the doll's black button eyes and wide painted-on grin. She would never let Dusty and the boys find out she still slept with RagAnn, but she wasn't willing to give her up. Not yet.

"Night, RagAnn," Mink whispered and reached beside her bed to tug the little metal pull string that turned off her white milk-glass lamp, her arm brushing the fuzzy pink pom-pom balls Mom had glued to the bottom of the green shade.

In the darkness, she lay thinking about what the Wrangler brothers could have possibly seen in the woods. That's when she heard it: *Scritch, scritch, scritch*. The high-pitched scraping noise seemed to be coming from the window beside her bed. She typically felt safe and sound in her cozy bed because Mom and Dad had built a homemade canopy frame so she could hang curtains from the ceiling and down the sides of the bed. But she felt suddenly vulnerable in the dark. Her heart raced.

Scritch . . . surely it was a branch . . . *scritch* . . . it had been breezy that day . . . *screee-eee-etch*! Was it getting louder, more insistent? But tree branches didn't get insistent. Did they? Mink's mind suddenly emptied, and no thought came. Her skin felt prickly and hot, but she was too nervous to pull back the covers. Covers equaled safety, right? Especially when dealing with monsters?

Besides, she was probably being silly. She forced herself to glance toward the window. *Please let it be a branch please let it be a branch* . . .

But it didn't look like any branch she'd ever seen. Beneath the partially drawn shade, which Mom had also trimmed with fuzzy pink pom-poms, she saw the dark silhouette of an object. It looked like . . . a *hand*. No, not a hand. A *claw*. Mink's chest filled with a scream that stuck there, filling her lungs with its heat and dread until she thought they would burst. She pulled the bedspread over her entirely, ensuring that nothing was sticking out, including her toes. *Especially* her toes, which were known among children to be prime monster bait. She did a mental checklist up her body and noted everything was covered except the fingers that held the bedspread over her head. That couldn't be helped. Frantically, her mind searched for reasonable solutions to the noises. A claw-shaped branch. A claw-shaped piece of metal from the gutter Dad never fixed. A claw-shaped . . . claw. *A Wolf Woman claw*. Mink realized she was being silly because her window was at least four feet from the ground on the outside of the house and no wolf was four feet tall. Unless . . . *unless it stood on its hind legs*.

Her breath came fast and hot, quickly making her protective bedspread lair more humid than the wind coming from Mobile Bay in August. When no more scratching sounds came and her heart rate slowed, Mink pulled the covers down an inch at a time. Her room was just as it always was, and she could see nothing behind the window shade. Still, she turned on the lamp before settling back and pulling RagAnn closer. She must have finally fallen asleep because when she opened her eyes, it was morning.

When she came down for breakfast, Mink saw Dad sitting at the kitchen table eating his Wheaties and reading the *Mobile Press-Register* newspaper.

"Listen to this," Dad was saying to Mom. "According to dozens of frightened witnesses along Davis Avenue and Plateau, a strange creature, a half woman and half wolf, has been making nightly rounds of the Port City. Reportedly, the apparition first appeared near Davis Avenue about one week ago."

"Oh, Dan, stop," Mom interrupted. "You know how the Wrangler boys are. They were just making that up."

"But I'm reading this directly from the front page of the

newspaper," he insisted. "The story says both the police department and the newspaper offices received numerous calls about the sightings."

Ignoring Mom's skeptical look, he continued reading: "'It was like a woman and wolf, pretty and hairy.' said one worried witness." He continued reading eyewitness quotes: "'My daddy saw it down in a marsh and it chased him home,' reported a teenager, who added, 'Now, my mom keeps all the doors and windows locked.'"

"'The top half was a woman and the bottom was a wolf,' explained another witness. 'It doesn't seem natural,' he added."

"One woman said she understood the creature had escaped from a circus sideshow."

"Wow. That's nuts, right?" Dad said, then "Oh, hey, Doodle-bug," as he spotted Mink, quickly folding the newspaper and putting it down.

"Don't listen to Dad," Mom said, getting up to put some Pop-Tarts in the toaster and kissing Mink's head as she passed. "He's pulling our leg," she added as if, between them, they had only the one.

"Look!" Dad cried indignantly, once again holding up the front page and stabbing a drawing with his index finger. Mink sat in the seat beside him with Mom looking over her shoulder.

The drawing, right in the center, showed what could only be described as a Wolf Woman. Some artist's idea of one, anyway. The pen-and-ink sketch showed what was definitely the hind-end of a wolf with what could only be described as the upper body of a decidedly southern woman. She was using one delicate furred claw—*claw!*—to push aside the long, flowing hair that fell from her head over her shoulders. Actually, in the drawing, she looked kind of pretty and . . . *nice.*

37

Mrs. Devereaux was still skeptical, even with the newspaper article. "Well, that reporter may have really quoted those people but how do they know the so-called witnesses weren't joking? It is April, after all." She shook her head, brought Mink two Pop-Tarts on a plate and wandered back to the laundry room.

Mink didn't know what to think. Newspapers didn't print stories that weren't real. I mean, that had to be illegal or something, didn't it? On the other hand, her mom was right—it *was* April, the time for April Fool's Day jokes and pranks. She chewed her breakfast slowly and decided not to mention the noises that kept her awake. It actually seemed silly now, that she had been so frightened.

It wasn't until recess that she managed to get Dusty, Cleve and Bub-Eye together. They grouped beneath the domed monkey bars, Dusty speaking before they even sat on the sandy playground floor.

"Did you see the newspaper this morning?" he asked excitedly. They all nodded. Their parents had all been discussing the front-page story. "Y'all have to give—you just made up that stuff about the Wolf Woman, right?" No one responded. "I mean, right?" Dusty prompted again.

"We didn't make it up," Cleve said, looking determined. Bub-Eye nodded, still looking nervous and afraid.

"Awww, c'mon . . ." Dusty began but Mink put a hand on his shoulder to stop him.

"Did she look like the drawing?" she asked quietly.

"Well . . ." Bub-Eye hesitated. "She didn't have that look like she'd been to the beauty shop, like a mom or something. But she definitely had that long hair on her head and a long snout like a wolf."

Mink nodded, thinking of her fear the night before. She

decided, for some reason, not to mention it. Typically, she shared everything with her neighbors. Maybe she just didn't want to be labeled a chicken. Whatever the reason, she stayed silent.

She met Dusty after school to walk home as usual. The Wranglers went to Mrs. McRaney's house after class because Mrs. Wrangler worked as a secretary at the local radio station until 4:30 each day. As Mink and Dusty, walking more silently than usual, rounded the corner of their street, they saw yet another exciting scene—a police car parked in the cul-de-sac.

"What are they doing here?" Dusty asked.

Mink shrugged but her chest clenched. "Let's find out." She walked up to the police officers, who were standing outside their car talking with Mrs. Devereaux and Mrs. Rutledge. Their dads were all still at work.

"We don't know what to think either," one officer said. He looked young—like just-out-of-school young. "But when people call us, we have a duty to investigate. And, Lord, have we had *calls*."

The other officer, husky and tired looking, sighed. "I think it's just a case of mass hysteria," he said. "One person thinks they see something, then another one does, then another . . . there is no monster here. Obviously?" But that last part sounded more like a question to Mink.

"We're taking witness statements from everyone who called," Officer Baby Face said. "We were hoping to talk with the Wrangler boys since their mother called this morning."

It was news to the other moms, and to Dusty and Mink, that Mrs. Wrangler had made an official report. The night before, she'd brushed off the boys' claims as a prank.

"They won't be home until about 5:15 or so," Mrs. Deveraux said. "But you can find the boys over at Mrs. McRaney's."

The officers acknowledged Mink and Dusty only as they were returning to the patrol car, waggling their fingers and saying, "Hey, kids." Then, Officer Baby Face suddenly turned toward Mink and Dusty and asked, "You two didn't happen to see anything in the woods last night, did you?"

Mink was spared her answer. "Aww, leave 'em alone," Officer Husky said. "You'll just get more kids claiming they see monsters." Mink and Dusty entered their respective houses as the officers pulled away, and Mink settled in to do homework until it was time for dinner, even though it was Friday, so she wouldn't have to think about the monster that may be lurking behind her home.

After dinner, she watched television in the living room with her parents, staying up as late as she could. "C'mon, Doodle-bug," Dad finally said, shaking her shoulder. "Time for bed."

Mink hoped, as tired as she was, she would fall asleep before she even had time to think about the window by her bed. Still, she left the light on as she snuggled in with RagAnn.

"Night, Sweet Pea," Mom said.

"Night, Mama," Mink mumbled. Then she was asleep.

The light was off when Mink awakened in the night. Mom must have come in and turned it off after she fell asleep. Was that what woke her? She didn't think so. The house seemed quiet. Then she heard it: *scritch, scritch.*

Her body filled with a prickly heat, and she turned toward the window. The claw! She was sure she saw it, but it was gone as quickly as it had appeared. She lay still, listening. Her heart jumped when the cuckoo clock in the living room chimed but it was quickly followed by a warm flood of relief that it was a clock and not a Wolf Woman in her house. She was just about to talk herself into believing she imagined the noises and the claw

when she heard it again: *scritch, scritch*. This time the noise was muffled, coming from another room. Terrified but determined, Mink put her feet on the cool hardwood floor and crept to the family room. She stopped at the sliding glass door that led to the patio, pulled back the curtain and peeked out. It was too dark to see anything but the shadows of the woods at the edge of the yard. She flipped on the patio light and froze.

There, stopped in her tracks by the light, was a creature that looked like . . . well, a female werewolf. She didn't look like the drawing in the newspaper. She didn't look flirtatious or like a comic-book character. She looked . . . like a wild creature in search of dinner. Yet, the longer Mink looked into her eyes, the calmer Mink became. She was still filled with adrenaline—of course, there was a strange creature in her yard. But she wasn't *terrified*. At least, not like she had been. For some reason, she didn't feel she was in any danger, although that could have been the effect of being behind a closed and locked patio door.

Mink and the Wolf Woman watched each other for perhaps another fifteen or twenty seconds—the wolf's dark, marble eyes looking into Mink's blue ones—before the wolf suddenly bolted into the darkness of the forest.

Mink went back to bed and, exhausted, fell asleep.

In the morning, she'd planned to tell the boys and even her parents about what she'd seen. On her way to the breakfast table, she stopped and looked out the patio door. She watched the edge of the woods but saw no movement. She turned and headed for the breakfast table and opened her mouth to tell her parents what she'd seen when she heard Mom talking.

"Like I said before, I think it was just a prank," Mom said wisely. "You mark my words."

Mr. Devereaux was folding the paper. "Well, the police seem

to have put it to rest, anyway. They think maybe it was a wild dog or something. But now that the calls have stopped coming, we probably won't read any more about this Wolf Woman creature. Mornin', Doodles," Dad said when he saw her. "What do you have planned for this fine Saturday?"

Mink sat and poured milk on the bowl of Cap'n Crunch her mom set before her. "Not sure," she said. "Anything's possible."

"It sure is," Dad said. He stood and mussed her hair as he passed. "Your Mom and I, on the other hand, are going to plant flowers." He smacked Mom playfully on the rear and she gave a little jump and giggle.

Mink smiled and chewed her cereal. *Anything was possible.*

No one reported seeing the Wolf Woman after that. But sometimes, late at night, snug in her bed, Mink thought she heard a sound at her window. *Scritch, scritch, screeeetch.* When she did, she would cling to RagAnn, pull the covers to her chin and wait to fall asleep.

LEGEND 4

The Ghost Town of Praco

Heath knew he wasn't supposed to go near the abandoned mining town. He knew it was dangerous. He also knew it was illegal to trespass. He went anyway.

By the time he came back, he not only had to give a statement at the sheriff's office, but a patch of his dark hair had turned white. Other kids in the eighth grade started making fun of him and calling him "Skunk." They said his story couldn't possibly be true. They said he must have made the patch himself with bleach.

But if they knew the truth, they might not think what happened to Heath was so funny. What did happen, you ask?

Only Heath can say for sure and he's not talking any more. But he did provide a detailed incident report for the sheriff and write a school report that led him to go to the town in the first place.

If you're interested, here's the school report Heath wrote about mining history, although it is admittedly a little dry and light on details:

Class: Social Studies
Teacher: Mrs. Collins
Name: Heath Horton

In 1905, Pratt Consolidated Coal Company in Jefferson County built a mine pretty much in the middle of nowhere. They called the mine "Praco," from the first letters of the company's name.

Mines are dangerous places to work, and mining disasters were common back then. But people were desperate for work and Pratt Consolidated would eventually employ 1,700 people.

These people formed a community and the company decided to build housing for the miners and ended up building a whole town with a store, a doctor, a school, and a bunch of little houses. Soon, the town (also called Praco) had 600 houses where miners and their families lived.

I found a bunch of disaster and mining websites on the internet with information about some of the bloody incidents that happened at the mining town. Below are a few:

1915: Dr. C. Clifton Ferrell, president of the West Pratt Coal Company who lived in Praco, was shot and killed by two men who were trying to burglarize the company store. The store was located right beside Dr. Ferrell's house. (Source: *Coal Age* magazine, 1915)

1938: A rock roof inside a shaft collapsed inside the mine. Nine men were trapped. Six of them died. (Alabama Mining accidents, 1891–1999)

1943: An explosion inside the mine left ten miners dead. It was supposedly caused by a spark from a coal-cutting machine that ignited a pocket of methane gas (see Robert H.

Woodrum's 2007 book *Everybody Was Black Down There: Race and Industrial Change in the Alabama Coal Mines*).

1981: The mine closed in the 1950s but some people still lived in the mining houses. In 1981, the company threw people living in the last eighty homes out on the streets. Many had nowhere to go. After they left, everything was torn down except for the huge silos that were used to store the coal.

In conclusion, although coal was necessary for fuel back then, getting the coal out of the ground was extremely dangerous and many people died while trying.

The paper was graded a "B-" with a notation from the teacher: "Interesting details but too short! I assigned 500 words."

The police report gave more details of the mining town:

Report of Heath Horton on a trespassing incident in the old Praco mining town:

I didn't think I'd survive, if you wanna know the truth about it. You can punish me all you want but I already learned my lesson: I will never go anywhere near that place again—or any abandoned or off-limits place.

You asked if I tried to get inside the mine. Of course, I didn't. One shaft is 3,000 feet deep. One slip and—bam!—you have exited the world of the living. Besides, it's locked up.

And I did go by myself, which was stupid, I guess. I thought I would just walk around to see if anything was left of the town. I got interested in it when I wrote a paper for school. I mean, people call it a ghost town and I'd never seen one. I just wanted to see if anything was still there.

I went early this morning, about nine, I guess. In summer, my mom usually lets me ride my bike over to my friend Robert's house, so that's where she thought I was going. I didn't tell her otherwise.

Really, it was hard to see much at all at first. The weeds were all grown up. In some places, the entire ground was covered, and I had to walk around that patch and find another way to keep going. I'm kinda scared of walking through big patches of kudzu, or whatever, in the woods because there might be a snake in there. Or one of those gigantic wolf spiders. They creep me out.

After a while, I found some areas without so many weeds and vines. I kept watching the ground. Finally, I could see the outlines of what used to be the roads in the town. They were dirt roads, red dirt, and then I found these rocks that looked like little pieces of very thin, brittle glass plates. Slate, that deputy said when he picked me up. It was everywhere.

I followed a few of the roads that were cleared enough but didn't find anything, except for a small dirt-covered piece of metal I saw alongside one of the roads. I picked it up. I couldn't tell what it was because it was so dirty. I spit on it and wiped it with my shirt.

It was a metal tag of some sort. It had the number 57 stamped on it. I put it in my pocket.

It was then I saw a big, wooded area with huge pine trees. I saw this huge shadowy shape beneath the trees and nearly jumped right out of my skin. It rose toward the sky, as big as a three-story building. The thing looked like a stone tower from a castle. It was about halfway covered in kudzu vines. It looked like it was being eaten by vines. Then I realized it was a silo where coal was stored back in the day. I'd seen photos of similar structures while doing research for Mrs. Collins's class.

I started making my way to it. I was really scared to step into the deep vines, but this castle thing just drew me to it.

I was about, oh, I guess, forty feet from the castle thing when I heard an odd whispering sound. I mean, I couldn't make out words or anything. I figured it was the wind.

I took another couple of steps and then I heard the noise again. This time I thought the whisper said, "You don't belong here." I froze. My heart was thumping like a car playing bass through those giant speakers . . . you know what I mean? I was shaking like one of those booming cars, too.

I felt like my tennis shoes were superglued to the ground. I just couldn't make them move. Like playing freeze tag, only this was real.

Just then I saw like a grayish-black cloud come from around the side of the castle-silo thing. I thought to myself "It isn't supposed to rain today." Then the cloud began to form a shape, first it was sorta tornado-like. You know, funnel shaped? But then—I don't care if you believe me or not—it took the shape of a man. A man with a bright spot right in the center of where his head-shape was. I was just about to have a talk with my feet to get them to move when the man-shape came at me. I mean, it came like an F-15 fighter jet. I thought it would hit me and was about to duck, but it flew straight over my head, ruffling my hair on the way past.

My feet really came unglued at that point! I took off. I didn't care about snakes or wolf spiders or anything else. I just needed to get away from that man-shape. My mind had not given it any other name than that.

I had put some distance between me and the silo when I felt, like, this huge explosion of pain in my toe as it struck a stone. My body continued half running, half flying in the air until I landed on a piece of concrete foundation. I skidded across it, and I knew my knee was going to be shredded.

I sat up to look at the damage and saw blood begin to bead from the scrapes on my knee. It stung but I really wanted to get out of there, so I stood and put my weight on it. I figured it would be okay until I got home.

That's when I noticed: I hadn't hit concrete from the ruins of an old house or building. I'd hit a granite slab covering a grave!

I looked around. Headstones jutted up through the kudzu. I was in a cemetery. I didn't see too many headstones—about eleven, I think—but I knew there were probably more graves that weren't marked.

I wondered, "Is this where the miners and their families were buried?"

Anyhow, I was standing there wiping dirt from words etched on the headstone so I could see the name and forgot the man-shape—I know, right? How can you forget something like that?

Suddenly, it was on me, with the spot on its head shining through the woods.

Had it followed me? By then, I'd realized it was a ghost. Laugh if you want, but that's the only way to describe it. I started to back away but then there was another grayish-black shape with a shining spot on its head. Then there was another and another and another until I was surrounded. I don't know how I managed to count with the panic that filled my brain, but I think there were six of them.

The Boy Scouts don't teach you what to do when surrounded by ghosts. Should I say something? Maybe they were friendly—you know, like Casper? All of a sudden, I could *feel* anger. I don't know how, but I knew I was feeling the spirit's anger. The air was hot . . . and itchy-like.

I was looking at the ghosts, trying to find a place where I could run between them. I had no idea what would happen if I tried to run *through* one of them.

Then the first ghost, the one that followed me, seemed to float over to a headstone and stare at me.

What did it want? I had no clue. My knees were shaking, and I thought I'd soon fall down.

Ghost No. 1 then flew away from the headstone and then back again. It hovered there.

"Do you want something?" I asked it.

The ghost nodded. The anger I'd felt wasn't quite as hot now. Maybe if I helped it, it would let me leave.

I thought maybe the headstone had a clue. I pushed the vines away from the stone and tried to read the name on it. It was too dirty. I pulled off my T-shirt and used it to wipe the dirt from the name.

"Willie," I said. The ghost nodded. "J . . . I can't read the last name. It's all cracked." The ghost didn't move so I went back to clearing the stone.

There, under the name, was a small etching. It looked like a number.

"Fifty-seven," I read aloud.

Ghost No. 1 swooshed around almost like it was . . . I don't know . . . *excited*. That's when I remembered the tag I'd picked up. I still didn't know what it was. Some kind of miner ID, like a military dog tag?

I pulled it from my pocket and sensed anger again from my ghost, who I now believed was the spirit of Willie J.

The other five ghosts surrounded me, as I stood beside Willie's grave holding the tag. "Was this yours? Are you Willie?"

The ghost nodded.

"And you want it back?"

The ghost nodded.

I carefully laid the number 57 tag on the grave of Willie J. "There," I said.

The anger level had subsided quite a bit. I realized these must be the spirits of the miners killed in the roof collapse, or maybe in an explosion. If so, they had a right to be angry. Just then, it came to me that the spots on their heads were their miners' lights. Or ghost miners' lights.

Anyhow, the spirits made room in the circle for me to walk through. They were letting me leave.

I put my shirt back on. Slowly, I began to walk between them toward the opening they made. When I was outside the circle, I turned around one last time. There was nothing there.

I'm not kidding. They were all gone. But I swear to you: They were there!

Whether the police believed young Heath's tale is hard to say, but one thing's for sure: Heath will never go back there. He has a reminder of his strange day at Praco: a patch of his dark hair had somehow been bleached almost a pure white, right in the center above his forehead. It looked, at least to those who knew Heath's tale, just like a glowing miner's light.

LEGEND 5

They Saw the Light at the Redmont

"**M**y most memorable vacation?" JoLynn asked Mrs. Pendergast, repeating the question her teacher had just asked and giving herself a moment to think. It wasn't that she didn't know which was her most memorable vacation. There was no question about that. It was whether she wanted to tell the story in front of the whole tenth-grade public speaking class.

JoLynn took a deep breath and decided to go for it. They'd either believe her or they wouldn't, she thought, as she walked to the front of the classroom. Either way, they were about to get a good story.

It was two years ago. It was me, my mom and dad, and my little brother, Jackson, who was twelve then. We were driving to my grandmother's house in Georgia, and we decided to spend the night in Birmingham so Mom and Dad could see a show at the Alabama

Theatre. Mom looked up all the hotels nearby and noticed a story about the Redmont. She loves history, so she booked a suite.

Maybe Mom loves history a little too much. She started looking up stories about the Redmont two weeks before we even left on the trip. "It was built in 1925," she told us. And then mom said, "Plus, it's haunted."

She noticed several classmates' heads bob like they'd been about to doze off until they heard the word "haunted." Even Mrs. Pendergast perked up, moving her chair a little closer.

Mom was smiling, and I knew she didn't believe what she was saying. She has never believed in ghosts and spirits. She added: "At least, that's what this one website says. I don't put much stock into that kind of thing, but apparently it's haunted by more than one ghost. Isn't that fun?"

My brother didn't look so sure. I didn't say anything, but it sure didn't sound fun. When we pulled up at the Redmont, Jackson and I were pretty disappointed. "It doesn't look haunted," Jackson said. I agreed. Where was the sloping roof and porches covered in cobwebs? The Redmont was just a tall, blocky building going up many floors.

But it was pretty cool inside. I knew Mom thought it was awesome. She wouldn't shut up about it. "Look at that chandelier," she whispered in the lobby, looking up to see the crystal chandelier that hung from two floors above. There were velvet sofas, and glittery silver on one wall. We saw this crazy-cool spiral staircase, but Dad said we were taking the elevator because we had too many bags to take up. We weren't going all the way to the top, of course. Our suite was on the fifth floor. It had two big beds, one for Mom and Dad and one for me, and Jackson would sleep on the pull-out sofa bed.

When we finally got inside the room—which was freezing cold with the AC blasting—I flopped on the bed farthest from the door because Mom liked to sleep closest to the bathroom, for some reason. I thought she was finished talking about the hotel but, no. She set down her suitcase and immediately picked up a brochure on the table. She started reading. "Did you know when the hotel opened it was billed as 'Birmingham's Most Modern Hotel?' Each room had a private bathroom, which was really rare back then."

"Oh, honey!" Mom squealed to Dad as she kept reading the brochure. "Guess what! Hank Williams Sr. stayed here the night before he died. I wonder if he stayed in this room. That's really fascinating. Isn't that fascinating, kids?"

"Who's Hank Williams Sr.?" Jackson and I said in unison.

Mom shook her head. "Really? Don, the kids don't know who Hank Williams is."

"I heard," Dad said from the bathroom.

Mom set out to correct the omission in our education. "He's only one of the most legendary country singers of all time. And he was born right here in Alabama," Mom said. Then she had to explain the entire life of Hank Williams Sr., which turned out not to take long because he was only 29 years old when he died. She just said he wrote a bunch of famous songs in the 1950s—one was called "Hey, Good Lookin'," which sounds corny. Then on New Year's Eve, like in 1952, some guy was driving Hank Williams to a concert when, in the middle of the night, he realized Hank wasn't sleeping—he was dead! Without his driver realizing it, Williams had died quietly during the trip. Anyway, Mom said the car he was riding in is on display in a museum in Montgomery, which sounds downright gruesome to me.

It was sad, sure, but it's hard to get too broken up over something that happened a literal lifetime ago. We all got settled in and rested a bit, then Mom and Dad got dressed. Dad ordered a pizza for me and Jackson, then Mom and Dad left for the show. We pulled out the sofa bed and, when the pizza came, we put a towel on the bed and ate right there while we watched an old movie, *The Thing from Another World*. I went to the bathroom during a commercial and when I came back Jackson was white as a, well, a ghost. "What, did the movie scare you?" I asked, but he was looking toward the closet rather than at the TV, a slice of pizza drooping in his hand.

"The closet door just opened by itself," he said, his voice slightly trembly. I looked from him to the closet and back again. "*Suuure*," I said. "Very funny." But Jackson wouldn't budge from his story, and he sounded pretty serious. I know it's a cliché, but I told him it must have been a draft. He looked at me. "Do you feel any drafts?" He had me there.

We went back to watching the movie and when it was over, I told Jackson to get into PJs and brush his teeth. Then I went into the bathroom and took a quick shower. When I got out, I pulled on my bathrobe and then noticed the mirror was covered in steam. I was about to wipe it with the sleeve of my robe so I could see myself when letters began to form in the mirror, as if written by an invisible finger.

At this point everyone in the class began chattering. "No way!" "You gotta be kidding;" "Who ya gonna call?" and "Awww, come on!"

"Class, let's be quiet," Mrs. Pendergast said and turned to JoLynn. "JoLynn, don't you think this speech is too . . . er, scary . . . for this class? Perhaps you should stop."

The chatter started up again but this time students were saying: "You can't stop now!" "This is just getting interesting."

Mrs. Pendergast sighed and said "Continue."

Where was I? Oh, yeah, the mirror. I watched as the letters took form in the foggy mirror. I'm telling you the truth. And pretty soon I could see the words "I" and "saw." My heart was fluttering like I had a hummingbird trapped in my chest. I couldn't think. I couldn't move.

I called to Jackson to come in there. "What now?" Jackson said, annoyed, as he entered the bathroom. "*Invasion of the Body Snatchers* is coming on . . ." His voice trailed off as he looked at the mirror, too. By now the message said "I," "saw," and "the."

"H—h-how is that possible?" Jackson whispered, as the invisible finger added an L.

"I have no idea," I whispered back. My feet seemed glued to the floor. More letters came: I, then G.

"Should we call for help?" Jackson said, his voice so low I could barely hear him. Then there was an H, and now a T.

"Light." I ignored Jackson's question. "I saw the light." No more letters appeared and soon the mist cleared from the mirror. For a minute we couldn't speak. My knees were shaking, which I hoped Jackson couldn't see under the robe. I needed to act as if I wasn't scared. "I wonder what it means."

"Who cares what it means?" Jackson said. "Let's get out of here!"

Once my thundering heartbeat had slowed, I was able to think about this. Maybe it was a prank someone found on TikTok. Maybe someone made those letters in Vaseline or something before they left so the mist wouldn't stick to those areas. But that didn't explain how we saw them appear so gradually, as if someone were writing them. I took a deep breath. "Mom and Dad would kill us," I said. "I'm sure it was just a joke." I explained my theory.

Jackson nodded. I'm sure he didn't buy that explanation, but it did calm him down. "It's over now," I said. "Let's go watch the movie."

"Are you sure?" Jackson said.

"Sure I'm sure," I said, knowing my tone sounded far from sure. "I'll stay out there with you until Mom and Dad come home." I pulled on some shorts and a T-shirt to sleep in and looked at the clock. Only eight-thirty. Ugh. At least Jackson was absorbed in the movie, although he made me sit on the bed with him rather than in the chair. I was sitting cross-legged on the sofa bed, studying my phone. I had googled "Redmont Hotel" and "haunted." There were so many entries! Lots of people had claimed to see ghosts at the Redmont.

I was a little afraid at this point to continue my research since I was pretty sure I was, you know, actually *in the haunted hotel*. But I overcame it and kept going.

The writer of the first entry wrote that she saw doors open and close on their own . . . at that point I couldn't help but look at the closet door. It was closed now. "Jackson, did you close the closet door?" Sounding annoyed at the interruption, Jackson said, "No. Why . . . ?" He stopped when he saw the closed door. "Who closed it?" he asked, sounding panicked. I could suddenly feel him right up next to my side like a baby monkey on its mama.

The class giggled at that.

I didn't want to scare Jackson more, so I said maybe I'd closed it without thinking. He looked doubtful but eventually went back to the movie, although he didn't scoot away from my side one bit. Mom and Dad wouldn't be home until midnight, and I didn't want to bother them on their night out. I didn't know what else to do except try to keep Jackson calm. I thought about calling the front desk on that little phone they keep in the rooms, but I figured they would think I was bonkers. I went back to my search.

I found a blog post. The writer claimed that during his stay his luggage moved from where he initially set it. He wrote: "That's when I saw a figure take shape. It was a man dressed as he would have been in the 1940s. I knew right away this was Clifford Stiles, who was the owner back then." I shivered and continued reading. I learned Clifford didn't die in the hotel. He died elsewhere in the 1970s. *Why would he come back to haunt here, then?* I wondered. This is probably just a hoax.

Just then we heard a slam, and, in unison, we grabbed each other. It sounded like it came from the bathroom, which was in the bedroom area of the suite. We couldn't see it from where we sat. I could feel Jackson trembling and he was making these little noises, kinda like a kitten. Don't tell him I told y'all that. He'd be so mad. Anyhow, I was too afraid to put my feet down on the floor, too afraid to move. We sat there, clinging to each other and frozen, looking into the opening into the bedroom. That's when we saw it. This smoky-looking shape. We watched as the shape took form and before long, we could see it was a man… because it *was* a man, just not one that was alive.

Several people in class gasped, including Mrs. Pendergast. "What did you do?" someone called. "I would have peed my pants," said another, earning a disapproving glance from Mrs. Pendergast.

All of a sudden, it was like I came unstuck, unfrozen. I could finally move. That's when I called the front desk and asked for help, like from a security person or something. When someone knocked on the door, we were still huddled on the sofa bed. I was almost too afraid to get up and answer it, but I knew I had to. This woman came to the room—she was only in her twenties—and started asking questions and looking around. When we told her what we saw, she smiled. "You two haven't been watching scary movies, have you?" When she noted *Body Snatchers* on the TV screen, I knew she'd never believe us. After a short lecture about making fake calls to the security office, she left.

"Well, that was no help," I said to Jackson.

"She acted like we don't have brains just because we're kids. But it doesn't matter. I don't want to stay here," Jackson replied.

"Me either. But where else are we going to go without Mom and Dad, at night? You just lie down and go to sleep on the sofa bed, and I'll stay right here beside you keeping guard until Mom and Dad come home."

"Promise?" he said. "If you even go to the bathroom, I'm coming with you."

"Deal," I said.

Jackson was so tired from being so scared, he finally fell asleep. I couldn't have slept if I tried. As I sat there, I tried to pay attention to the TV, which had started airing *Wild Kingdom*—no more scary movies—but my ears perked when I heard a scratching noise. I toggled the volume down and listened. *Scritch, scritch.*

She tried making the sounds for the class. They were all hushed, waiting to see what happened.

I thought it was coming from the main door to our room! I got up and grabbed the iron from the closet, the only thing I could find that was heavy. Then I heard a *scritch* and a *clack* and the door opened! I raised the iron and... It was Mom and Dad.

Several of the students laughed in relief and let out their pent-up breaths.

Before they could ask about the iron, I grabbed Mom, then Jackson woke up and grabbed Dad.

"Wait a minute," Dad said, laughing. "Hold on. Did you miss us that much?" Then Jackson and I both started talking at once, trying to tell them what happened.

"Slow down," Mom said. She sat on the foldout bed. "Take some breaths and start again. JoLynn first." After we both described everything we heard and saw, Dad said, "Were you two watching horror movies?" I rolled me eyes at him. "Really, Dad? You don't believe us either?"

"Oh, come on," he said. "Y'all must have just fallen asleep after a scary movie and dreamed this. This hotel is not haunted."

Mom and Dad went toward the bedroom to change into their pajamas when suddenly, we heard faint music.

"Is the radio on?" Dad asked. "No? Are you kids watching You-Tube videos?"

"Wait!" Mom said. "That's 'I Saw the Light.' That's a Hank Williams song."

Jackson and I looked at each other. The words in the mirror!

Then Mom said, "Don, look!"

We stood behind Mom and Dad to see what she was pointing at. Then we saw the shape of a man, faint at first and then with more detail. He was clearer this time. He seemed fully formed, if transparent. It or he was holding a guitar and wearing a cowboy hat. His see-through hand strummed the guitar, seemingly in time to the music. Then the music and the figure began to fade at the same time. The cowboy-person tipped his hat and smiled, then he was gone.

Mom stood there, her finger still pointing to the spot where the man had been.

"That, that was Hank Williams!" Mom said incredulously. "He's been dead over seventy years. The kids were telling the truth!"

I thought Mom was going to fall down but she grabbed the back of a chair and stayed upright. I'd never seen Dad looked so scared. He was actually trembling. Then we all began talking at once. At one point, Jackson said, "We need to leave!" He was practically crying… don't tell him I said that, either. That got Dad's attention. He looked like someone just waking up, but he straightened his shoulders and told Jackson to sit on the edge of one of the big beds.

"Look, son," he said. "What we just saw scared me too, at first. I've never seen anything like it, and I can't explain it. But… I think this is a friendly ghost. Somehow, I just know we're not in any danger. But you can sleep with mom and me anyway." Jackson still wasn't too sure, but he was fine once he snuggled in with Mom and Dad. I slept in the second bed next to them and I kept my eye on the bathroom door. I finally fell asleep.

The next morning, in the daylight, everything seemed fine. None of the things we saw the night before seemed real. At the checkout desk, the clerk guy said, "How was your stay?" Dad said, "Great." We all smiled at each other because now we had a secret. Then the guy said "Did you know this was the last hotel Hank Williams ever stayed at? He died the next night." We all laughed and said in unison, "We know!"

JoLynn walked back to her desk, and her classmates actually applauded and whistled. A couple of the guys patted her on the back. Although JoLynn was sure that Mrs. Pendergast didn't believe a word of the story, the teacher still said, "Good job. I'll give it an A."

The Mysterious Last Voyage of the *Gloria Colita*

She cut through the waters of Mobile Bay with ease. The lines of the large vessel were classic and dignified. Wind pushed her sails, hanging from three masts, making a paintable scene against the setting sun. She even looked a bit blurred around the edges, as if rendered in watercolor.

Amelia made her observations silently, her eyes following the wooden ship curiously. Her attention snapped back when she heard her friend's voice.

"The sunset is going to be gorgeous from here," Lila was saying to Cecil, who was sitting in the booth beside her at the small-but-legendary Fish Camp Restaurant, just outside of Mobile. Amelia, Lila's best friend, was sitting with her date, Emmett. The group of young people was waiting impatiently on their orders—especially Cecil, who had been craving the famous fried catfish and hush puppies. That craving was the reason they came home from college for the weekend in the first place.

It was worth it, though. From their table they could see across

Mobile Bay and watch sailboats and ships until the sun disappeared into the horizon.

Amelia had turned her gaze back to the water. "Isn't that ship pretty? Especially with the bursts of pink-and-orange sky behind her. I wonder what she's called." Her forehead wrinkled. "There's something different about her. She looks almost unreal."

The boys looked out the window. "Can you make out the name?" Emmett asked Cecil.

"In this light and at this distance it's hard to see," Cecil said. "I think there's a G. Wait . . . *Gloria* . . . *Gloria* something. That's kind of a weird name for a ship."

"Nah. Most ships are named for women," Lila said.

Amelia nodded. "My grandpa was in the navy. He taught me to refer to ships as 'she.'"

"It's gone!" Lila said suddenly. "It, or *she*, just disappeared."

The others followed her gaze. The ship was nowhere to be seen.

Just then, a middle-aged woman who reminded Amelia of her Aunt Pearl arrived with their meals and began to set them on the table. "Let's ask her," Cecil said. "I bet she knows."

The woman, who'd introduced herself as Lavette, had set their meals on the table and was about to head back to the kitchen with her serving tray. "Hey, we saw a ship out there," Emmett said. "It was called *Gloria* something."

Lavette stood still, looking toward the window and the slowly darkening sky. Nothing was visible in the bay now.

"Three masts?" Lavette asked. "A schooner?"

"I don't know what a schooner is, but that sounds about right," Lila said.

"You saw the *Gloria Colita*," Lavette said in a hushed tone. "Not many people get to see her. I've never even seen her."

"Why? She's not from around here?" Emmett asked.

"No," Lavette said. "She's not from around here. She's not from anywhere."

Amelia looked confused. "What do you mean? She has to be from somewhere."

"I guess you haven't heard the stories," Lavette said. "I've been hearing them all my life."

"What stories?" asked Emmett.

"That wasn't a ship you saw out there. That was a ghost," Lavette said matter-of-factly.

"*Ghost*?!" Emmett and Amelia said at once. Lila's jaw dropped. They had so many questions. Except for Cecil, who was already eating his catfish and wasn't paying attention.

"A ship can't be a *ghost*," Emmett said.

Lavette only smiled.

"Oh, they can be," she said. "See, the term 'ghost ship' can mean a *real* abandoned ship, one everyone can see. If you find a vessel without anyone aboard, that's a ghost ship. But it can also refer to a *ghost ship*."

She emphasized that last part, but the kids were still confused.

"I mean a ship that is there, but it isn't really there, get me? You can see it, but it has no real substance. There's actually lots of 'em out there . . . it's a mighty big ocean. Like the *Mary Celeste*. She was discovered abandoned in 1872. Her eight crew members as well as the captain, his wife, and little daughter were nowhere in sight."

"I'm going to have nightmares," Amelia said, and shivered.

"The one good thing about ghost ships . . ." Lavette said. "They can't come on land." Then she walked away.

Amelia turned to the window. The light had faded until she could only see her reflection in the glass. What they hadn't mentioned to Lavette was that the four of them were going out in the bay in a cabin cruiser the next day.

Emmett noticed Amelia's face. "Oh, come on, Amelia. That's just a story."

"I don't believe in things like that," Lila said, dipping a hush puppy in ketchup and popping it in her mouth. "She was trying to scare us."

Cecil, who had torn through his meal, pushed his plate aside and said, "I'll google it while you eat."

"Here's a good entry," he said minutes later. "I'll read it to you." This is what they heard:

On February 4, 1940, the Coast Guard traced a ship, the *Gloria Colita*, after it was reported that she didn't return to port. She was located, adrift, about 150 miles from the Port of Mobile. Gaining access, the search party found the ship severely damaged. The masts were broken and the sails were ripped. The rudder was missing. They searched below deck for any of the *Gloria Colita* crew. They found no one. The ship was towed back to Mobile.

The *Southeast Missourian* newspaper reported at the time, "Found adrift in the Gulf of Mexico, rudderless without a shred of rigging, the British three-masted schooner *Gloria Colita* was towed to port in Mobile, Alabama."

The *Gloria Colita* was 165 feet long, counting the bowsprit. She had been carrying a load of lumber from Mobile to Guantanamo Bay in Cuba. The *Gloria Colita* had nine men aboard, including the captain. She was captained by her builder, Reg Mitchell of Bequia. Bequia, an island in the Grenadines, was known for its shipbuilding craftsmen, as was the Mitchell family. Reginald Mitchell followed in his father's footsteps but wanted to make a name for himself. In 1939, he set out to build the largest ship ever built in the Lesser Antilles.

When completed, his ship weighed 174 tons and was, indeed, the largest ever built on the islands. Her size seemed apropos since her captain was also oversized, reportedly standing seven feet tall. Mitchell named the ship for his daughter, Gloria Colita Mitchell, who was born in 1932.

Mitchell then put his cherished creation into service. The *Gloria Colita* hauled sugar, rice, and lumber between Miami, Cuba, and Venezuela. The ship had sailed from Mobile on January 21, 1940, but never made her destination. After the wreck was discovered, the Coast Guard crew boarded her and tried to uncover the reason for her abandonment. Most marine experts postulated that the ship was struck by a wave, possibly one as large as 100 feet high, and everyone on the ship was washed overboard and drowned.

Amelia gasped, nearly choking on a piece of fish. "Oh, how sad!" she said.

"There's more," Cecil said, scrolling down his phone to scan the last of the entry. "Hey, this is cool," Cecil said, then continued reading aloud.

A few people, however, speculated that the curse of the Bermuda Triangle led to her demise. The Bermuda Triangle, also known as the Devil's Triangle, has long been known as a dangerous place for seagoing vessels, as well as airplanes, which cross it. Many

disappearances have been recorded and attributed to the triangle—
including the infamous *Flight 19* and the USS *Cyclops*. *Flight 19* was a
group of five bombers that took off from Fort Lauderdale on Decem-
ber 5, 1945. One of the pilots reported a malfunctioning compass
and then the planes disappeared from radar. Five pilots, thirteen
crewmembers, and the planes were never seen again. In March 1918,
the USS *Cyclops* was sailing for Baltimore, Maryland, but she never
arrived. None of her 305 crew or the ship itself has ever been found.

The triangle is most popularly thought to be between Miami,
Puerto Rico and Bermuda, which is not near the *Gloria Colita*'s path.
Some, however, believe the cursed area has wider borders or that
perhaps the *Gloria Colita* had just reached the triangle when her
crew mysteriously disappeared.

Cecil held up his phone. "Look at this photo of the *Gloria Colita*.
The caption says it shows 'tangles of rigging, broken masts and
ripped sails'. Later she was used for scrap."

The four of them stared in silence for a moment, thinking
about the great mystery.

Then Emmett said, "Wait . . . what? She was scrapped? There
is no ship anymore?"

"Not according to this," Cecil said, holding up his phone.

"But we saw her," Amelia said. "Right out there." She pointed
to the now black window.

"And she was all torn up when they found her," Emmett said.
"Why did she look like new when we saw her?"

"Maybe it was a replica," Lila said. "I've seen those kinds of
ships before, like the *Niña*, *Pinta*, and *Santa Maria* replicas we
toured for school."

"Yeah," Amelia said. "That must be it." She turned back to the window and stared into the darkness.

The next morning, the two couples were on the boat, cutting through the waters of Mobile Bay, faces to the sun, hair blowing, ghost tales forgotten. Cecil was driving the rented cruiser. They couldn't hear one another over the sound of the engine so they mostly gazed out at the water.

As lunchtime neared, Lila tugged Cecil's sleeve to get his attention. "I'm hungry," she said loudly. "And hot!"

Cecil slowed the boat and turned off the engine.

"Let's eat then," Cecil said.

They started, one-by-one, for the narrow steps to the cabin when Amelia gasped. "What?" Emmett asked. She could only point.

There, across the water, was the *Gloria Colita*.

They all stood, staring. "I didn't think we'd see it in the daytime," Cecil said. "What's that on the deck? I thought I saw something move." He got his binoculars from the compartment under his seat and looked again.

"I can't believe it," he said.

"What is it?" Lila said, squinting in the direction of the ship. Cecil just stood, slack-jawed, and handed her the binoculars. She gasped and handed them to Amelia who handed them to Emmett.

"Is that what I think it was?" Lila whispered.

"It can't be," Emmett said.

"But it was," said Amelia. "I think that was Captain Mitchell . . . or at least his spirit."

"Maybe we should head home," Emmett said. Amelia nodded in agreement. "Did you see his eyes? They were black . . . like, bottomless. Soul-less."

The young people huddled in a circle on the deck and began talking at once.

"We need to get out of here . . ."

"Can you believe . . ."

"I want to go home . . ."

"No way! We're not going back," Cecil said. "Do you know how much this boat cost? We rented it for the whole day."

"Look!" Emmett said suddenly. Everyone stopped talking. Cecil turned his eyes up to the ship once more. "Hey! It's gone!"

"The captain?" Amelia asked, leaning over the deck railing to peer out over the water. Then she saw what he meant.

"All of it! It's all gone, the ship, the captain, everything," she said.

The four stared open mouthed across the water, momentarily speechless.

"That decides it then," Cecil said finally. "We're staying. I mean, it's not going to come back . . ."

Amelia whirled to face him. "Are you crazy? We need to leave. Right now."

"We wouldn't see it twice in one day, right?" Cecil said. "We already rented the boat. Let's stay and have some fun."

Amelia objected. Emmett looked unsure. He kept picturing Captain Mitchell's eyes.

Lila joined in. "Oh, c'mon," she said. She didn't look scared anymore. "It's going to be fine."

"Let's eat," Cecil said, clapping his hands together. "Then everyone will feel better."

Emmett reached for Amelia's hand and reluctantly the group

went down the steps into the cabin where there was a small kitchen.

They had packed a picnic-style lunch in a cooler with sandwiches and chips and Cokes.

The conversation turned to normal topics as they each chose their favorite sandwich and chips.

Amelia felt only slightly better, but she told herself, *Maybe Cecil was right. Maybe it was over.*

Everyone sat down with a sandwich and the conversation lulled momentarily as they began to eat.

Suddenly, they heard a noise on deck.

"What was that?" Lila whispered.

It sounded like someone coming over the railing, like the water dripping down as if someone was trying to pull himself up. Then they heard the sound of footsteps on the deck. They seemed to be coming nearer. Everyone was holding their breath until finally Cecil said in an urgent whisper: "Grab a weapon!"

As quietly as possible, Emmett grabbed a knife from the kitchen drawer and handed Amelia an ice pick. Lila saw the emergency kit attached to the wall and reached in and got the flare gun. Cecil found a hammer under the bench seat around the table.

The steps came closer and closer. The group waited, weapons held aloft, their eyes never leaving the cabin door.

Suddenly, the door flew open, banging on the side of the boat. There, in the entryway, stood Captain Mitchell with his coal-black eyes, seeming to fill the entire cabin with his bulk. They all froze on the spot.

"Lila," Cecil yelled. "Shoot the flare!"

She raised the gun but had nowhere to aim it—the figure had disappeared as quickly as it appeared. The four of them stood stock still until their legs began to go numb. Finally, Cecil went up the steps to the deck. No one was there and there were no boats in sight. There was nothing to see but water.

After a moment, they all gathered shakily back on the deck, sandwiches forgotten.

Without saying a word, Cecil pulled out the boat key. "You better secure those drink bottles down in the cabin. I'm going to go fast." Before any of them could even get to the steps, he started the engine and turned toward home. Amelia was so relieved they were going back.

After all, ghost ships can't come on land.

LEGEND 7

The Ghost Train of
Old Railroad Bed Road

"**D**id you know there used to be a railroad here?" Ruth asked her cousin, Fawn, who was visiting from Missouri.

"Where?" Fawn asked, looking around.

"Right where we're standing," Ruth said. Fawn looked down at her feet, clad in shiny Mary Janes and frilly white socks. She had an aversion to getting dirt on her dresses and hoped Ruth, who was more adventurous, wouldn't take her anywhere too covered in briars or cobwebs.

"I don't see any tracks," Fawn said, still staring at the red-dirt ground surrounding her feet.

"That's because they were all pulled up about twenty years ago . . . like maybe in the 1930s or something. I don't know because I wasn't born until 1942."

"Then how do you know they were here?" Fawn asked reasonably. She was only nine, two years younger than Ruth.

"Big Mama told me once when she was remembering stories from her childhood. Y'all had moved away by then, but she liked to tell stories about the old home place. This was the store," Ruth pointed to a weathered clapboard building whose only customers now were weeds that grew taller than Ruth and a variety of the insects and wildlife that populated Alabama's summers. "This is a ghost town now."

As she said the words, everything grew quiet around them, as if Ruth's comment had startled the mockingbirds, frogs, and cicadas into silence. Fawn gave a little shiver. "Ghost town?"

"Don't worry, silly," Ruth said. "That just means it's abandoned." As if cued by Ruth, the world around them began to supply background noise again.

Ruth took her younger cousin's hand. Fawn lived with her family in Georgia and was visiting Ruth's house because their grandparents, Big Mama and Daddy Frank, were in town.

Ruth, happy to have a little cousin to boss around, began leading Fawn toward the graying building constructed in the style of old West stores. "I want to stay on the road," Fawn said hopefully. They had already walked a half-mile from Ruth's family's home in Toney.

"Don't be a ninny-baby," Ruth said.

As their small legs—Ruth's covered in scrapes and mosquito bites and Fawn's caramel-brown and unmarked—plowed through the weeds toward the store, Fawn noticed cockle-burrs attaching to her white socks and sighed in resignation.

As Ruth tugged at Fawn's hand, she continued to describe the little town at the crossroads of Old Railroad Bed Road, which had been known as the community of Dan. *It was a strange name for a town*, Fawn thought. *It was like naming a dog Bill or Ethel.*

But she remained silent, and Ruth continued her story:

In 1887, a rail line was planned from Tennessee to Mississippi to be called the Decatur, Chesapeake and New Orleans

Railway. The route was never completed, however, and managed to cover only 37 miles, including the crossroads at Dan. The line was purchased in 1893 as part of the Middle Tennessee and Alabama Railway but that company only built as far as the community of Jeff, near Huntsville in Madison County. The entire rail line was abandoned in 1929 and the tracks were removed a few years later. Hence the name "Old Railroad Bed" Road.

"Big Mama says there was a bad train wreck here one time, a long time ago, when she was a really little girl. It happened up that way, toward Dan Crutcher Road," Ruth said, pointing north.

The girls reached the front of the small store, where Ruth rubbed the glass of a window, one of the few remaining unbroken panes, and stood on tiptoe to see inside. Fawn stood silently, watching. Other windows, likely broken by boys throwing rocks, were covered with plywood.

It was a stifling day in August. The girls' dresses stuck to their backs like flies to the poisoned paper strips on Big Mama's back porch, but Fawn didn't complain.

As Ruth rounded the building, checking it for entrances, she told the story the way Big Mama had told it:

On a similarly suffocating August day in the late 1880s, the heat had the passengers on the crowded train wiping their brows and fanning themselves with anything handy. There was little room to move in the only passenger car, but riders were headed toward Mobile to spend time at the Gulf coast, so they focused their thoughts on salt-infused sea breezes rather than their current discomfort.

They had no way of knowing that among their number were

two men with nefarious plans. The men were carrying with them bills and gold coins stolen from a bank before they went on the run.

Their plans, vague in the retellings, had to do with hijacking the train to carry them to parts unknown where they could safely hide. When the wanted men approached the conductor at the helm of the steam locomotive, they found the six-foot, five-inch, 310-pound man blocking their way to the engine. The thieves, armed with a coal shovel from the tender car, took on the unarmed engineer, starting a full-on melee.

Whether someone pushed a lever during the brawl, no one knows. What happened next occurred too fast for anyone to react—the train's wheels were leaving the track. It was derailing! Nearby residents could hear muttered prayers and terrified screams right up until the train cars hit the bottom of the deep spring beside the tracks. When people arrived at the wreck, they found only twisted metal and human carnage. The crew members, fifteen of the passengers, and the two thieves either died in the crash or in the shallow water beside the tracks.

Fawn's eyes had grown round. She'd been so enthralled, she'd forgotten her clean dress and sat in a clearing by the store, right on a smooth spot of red dirt.

"What happened then?" she asked.

"Well, Big Mama said the little town of Dan survived for a while, with a small post office and general store, a grist mill, a sawmill, and some houses, including the one where Big Mama's family lived when she was a girl. This building was the store and the post office."

"That's such a sad story," little Fawn said, thinking of the people screaming as the train derailed. Then she stood and looked up at Ruth. "But I'm hot. Can't we go home and get a Nehi? Besides, I thought Big Mama and Daddy Frank were coming to your house tonight for some of that peach ice cream your mama was churning."

It has to be past 7 o'clock, Fawn thought. The sun had fallen low in the sky as the girls had roamed and talked and the punishing temperature began its retreat, if only by a degree or two. That's when Fawn learned of her cousin's grim plan.

"I just wanted to wait here until dark," Ruth said. "I was hoping we would see the ghost train."

"The what?!" Fawn screeched.

"The ghost train," Ruth said calmly. "I've come out here before with Yancy, but we've never seen anything. I've got to see it before he does." Ruth and her older brother, Yancy, had quite the sibling rivalry. While it sounded nightmarish to Fawn, Ruth thought being the first to see the ghost train was an important rite of passage.

"I'm not staying here to look for any ghost train," Fawn said, grabbing at the edge of Ruth's hem to stop her progress. Ruth just kept walking. Finally feeling defeated, Fawn followed her older cousin back to Old Railroad Bed Road and sat alongside it.

Ruth explained what she was looking for.

"The legend says people have seen the lights from the train up and down Old Railroad Bed Road, mostly near this spot right here. That's where the spring is deepest, although now it looks kind of like a ditch filled with water. Yancy told me that a couple of years ago, Mrs. Branch—she lived right over there—was cooking dinner on her stove when she heard a train whistle. It had been such a common sound for years that it didn't occur

83

to her at first that the train tracks had been pulled up. But the rumbling of train wheels clacking down the line grew louder and louder until she looked out the kitchen window. She couldn't see a thing. Windows rattled and dishes moved along the kitchen shelves from the vibration. Then she heard people screaming. She swore up and down she could hear people screaming and praying.

"That's when her little daughter, Tally, began to squeal. Her mom scooped her up and ran for the basement, just like they did when the big tornado hit here in 1913. When Mr. Branch got home, he didn't believe his wife heard the train. 'There aren't any tracks to carry a train,' he kept saying. 'And there's no such things as ghosts.' Mrs. Branch stood firm in what she'd heard and seen and felt. Within the year, they'd moved away."

Fawn was now fully terrified and opened her mouth to once again try to convince her cousin to walk her home when Ruth whispered urgently: "Do you see that?"

Pulled unwillingly, Fawn's eyes moved to where her cousin's gaze fell. An orb of light was floating down the road in the growing dusk.

"It's a car!" Fawn said, so relieved she nearly fell over. Hopefully it was Ruth's dad, Uncle George, coming to take the girls home for peach ice cream.

That's when they heard the unmistakable low grumble of train wheels and the lonely, floating notes of its whistle.

"What was that?" Fawn asked, her eyes once again growing huge.

"Don't worry," Ruth said, but she couldn't hide the tremor in her voice. The light was getting closer and closer. Both girls felt rumbling directly beneath their feet and, as if from a distance, they heard cries of terror. The cacophony rose, seeming

to grow closer. Suddenly, a powerful gust of wind blew back the girls' hair, forcing their eyes closed.

When they opened them again, the light was gone. There was no shaking, no screaming, no sound at all.

Ruth had a punishing grip on her little cousin's hand.

"T-t-that was the ghost train, wasn't it?" Fawn whispered.

"It'll be all right," Ruth insisted, although her legs were twitching like jumping beans. "Let's get home."

The girls were so unsteady on their feet, it took twenty minutes to walk the half mile home. Neither spoke.

When they could see the lights of the front porch, relief turned their jumpy, taut muscles to noodles of relief.

"There you are!" Big Mama said. "We've been wondering."

The girls' grandparents, both sets of parents, and Yancy were sitting on the metal porch chairs eating ice cream from Ruth's mom's Blue Willow soup bowls, although Daddy Frank ate from a Pyrex mixing bowl of considerable size.

"You know you're not supposed to be out after dark," scolded Ruth's mother, Mary Earl. The girls collapsed on the porch steps, unable to walk any farther.

"Don't you want some ice cream?" Uncle George asked.

Fawn and Ruth could only nod. The desire to brag to Yancy about the ghost train seemed to have left Ruth altogether.

As Fawn's mom went to get two more bowls, Daddy Frank said, "Say, did you girls feel that earthquake? The ground shook and the house groaned."

"C'mon, Daddy Frank," Yancy said to his grandfather. "You know we don't have no earthquakes around here. It must've been some kind of testing over at Redstone Arsenal. Maybe bombs or something like that."

"Did y'all hear a train whistle?" Fawn asked suddenly.

"A train whistle?" Yancy said with a laugh. "There ain't no train that comes through here no more."

"There used to be, though," Big Mama said. "Did I ever tell you about the time when a train crashed just right over yonder? It was a terrible thing . . ."

Ruth and Fawn glanced at each other, then busied themselves dipping some ice cream into their bowls. They already knew how Big Mama's story ended. They also knew there would be no sleep for them that night.

LEGEND 8

Who Killed Jethro Walker?

In a cemetery in Auburn, Alabama, a headstone and a bronze plaque serve as a reminder of a mystery that would be otherwise forgotten. Pine Hill Cemetery, established in 1837, is home to many of the city's deceased residents, who, for the most part, lie quietly in their coffins.

There are legends, though, told on dark nights around campfires, that perhaps not all Pine Hill inhabitants are content with their lot in death.

Pine Hill is a tidily landscaped burial ground near downtown Auburn, not far from the entrance to the campus of Auburn University, which was founded in 1856 as East Alabama Male College. Above the wrought-iron gates at the entrance is an arch that reads "Pine Hill."

There is more wrought iron inside the gates, forged into fences demarcating family plots—some with ironwork as elaborate as hand-sewn lace, others with pieces rusted and broken.

Pine Hill counts among its population early settlers and numerous well-respected university professors, researchers, and presidents. Many of the grave markers are simple slabs set into the ground, although more-decorative headstones and obelisks are sprinkled about the landscape. One grave is even marked with a figural memorial, the Italian marble statue of a kneeling little boy holding a lizard in a tray. The boy buried there was Charles Stodgill Miles, age eight when he died in 1937, who loved nature and whose father was a botanist at the university. Ironically, it was nature that killed little Charlie—he died of a reaction to an insect bite. The statue has been vandalized numerous times and has, for many years, remained headless (as has the lizard).

One of the largest monuments in the cemetery draws people to it. The white marker has a rectangular base topped with an obelisk. A relief on the base shows a laurel wreath; in the wreath's center is etched the name "Jethro Walker."

Below the name are these words:

Born in Putnam Co. Geo.
Feb. 18, 1808
Died in Macon Co. Ala
March 11, 1858

Each October, visitors gather for the Pine Hill Lantern Tour, on which actors play various historical characters. On those nights, the lanes in the cemetery are lined with luminaries that create an ethereal glow.

At one end of the cemetery, an actor stands in front of a brick tomb and portrays William Mitchell (1787–1856), a well-known figure in Auburn. He was born the son of a Revolutionary War officer. His claim to fame is that he was buried inside the tomb in his feather bed, with his slippers tucked beneath it.

At another point, an actor portrays Dr. Charles Allen Cary (1861–1935), founder of Auburn's famed veterinary college.

Then, a man dressed in clothing from the 1800s—except for his shoes, which are obviously a pair of solid black Adidas—stands beside Jethro Walker's obelisk to tell his story. But it's a story with no ending, giving rise to the legends claiming that the spirit of Jethro Walker has unfinished business on this earth.

On one such tour night, Jojo Cochran and her sister, Pip, were among the guests. Pip, only ten years old, was already nervous about walking around in a cemetery after dark, even though there were small groups of adults everywhere. She clung to Jojo's hand like a tick on a dog. As the girls approached the actor playing Jethro Walker, Jojo said: "I've heard this story. MaryLeigh told me about it when she slept over. She said his ghost is seen here in the cemetery sometimes, hovering around his grave."

Pip gave a whole-body shiver. "Really?" she squeaked.

Jojo had momentarily forgotten her sister's sensitivity to ghost stories—Pip read the *Goosebumps* books and believed every word.

"No, not really," Jojo said quickly. "It's just a story. Here, let's read what the plaque says." She read aloud:

Jethro Walker
(1808-1858)

An early settler of Auburn, Walker was killed by a bullet in his head while reading his Bible in his parlor with Mr. Dubberly. His murderer was never caught, but it was always very interesting that a son left rather quickly for Cuba soon afterward. The story goes that he had promised to whip his young son for disobedience, and the son beat him to the punch, with a more serious weapon. Walker was a lawyer, large plantation owner where he owned a home at Armstrong, and owner of a townhouse in Auburn. From his estate records from 1853-1858, he provided midwifery services for eighteen children born on his plantation. His is one of the tallest monuments in Pine Hill and two of his wives are buried in the English fashion, one on top of the other, next to him. His third wife outlived him.

The girls learned even more about Walker from the actor portraying him. His parents were Nathaniel L. Walker and Phoebe Browning Walker. The couple married in 1800 and went on to have twelve children, six boys and six girls.

Jethro Walker married a woman named Matilda and moved to Auburn at some point. That marriage lasted until her death in 1844. Jethro soon remarried, but his second wife, Mary Elizabeth Mims Walker, died in childbirth in 1846. His third wife, Martha Crittenden Walker, outlived her husband.

In his fifty years of living, Walker became a successful businessman, although the success of his cotton plantation was built on the backs of enslaved people. That was something JoJo thought was horrible, and she found it difficult to think of the man in the story as fully human when he bought and sold other humans. She knew it was a part of history that couldn't be rewritten, though, and she was intrigued by the mystery of the man's death.

Walker owned a plantation and a sawmill and was a pioneer of plank roads, which were toll roads built of wood. In the 1840s, plank roads were thought to be the transportation conveyance of the future, and Jethro became a founding partner in the Auburn to Tallapoosa Plank Road Company. The company built roads made from large pine logs sawed lengthwise and laid in rows, rounded side down. He was also one of the earliest commissioners of the town of Auburn, beginning his service there in 1842.

When the actor finished his talk, Jojo and several others in their small group murmured their "thank-yous" and the sisters began to walk toward the next site on the tour.

"I saw a plank road once," Jojo said as they strolled.

"A real one?" Pip asked.

"I think it was a replica," said Jojo. "You know, one they built to look like a plank road from the 1840s. We saw it on a school field trip to Tannehill State Park, where one was built to get to the Tannehill Ironworks back then. Mrs. Dalrymple said groups of rich men also planned plank roads for Tuscaloosa and Prattville."

"Why aren't there any now?" Pip asked. The idea of a wooden road seemed kind of neat. She remembered seeing one that crossed Clarkson Covered Bridge in Cullman, where she and her family had picnicked one day in the spring.

"Because after about five years, everyone figured out planks didn't do a very good job of supporting carriages," Jojo said. "People hoped they would work better than dirt roads that got all muddy when it rained, but I guess the planks just squished down into the mud. All the companies went out of business."

"And by then, that Jethro guy was already dead," Pip surmised.

"Yep," Jojo said.

Suddenly, Jojo stopped walking. She realized that she and Pip had reached a stand of trees and, away from the groups, were standing in darkness with only her lantern to light their paths.

Jojo turned to look back at Jethro Walker's grave, the last place they'd seen other people. The actor playing Jethro Walker was the only one still there, awaiting his next tour group.

"We'd better get back with the group," Jojo said. She and Pip, whose hand had relaxed slightly in hers, began walking toward the actor. He was standing in front of Walker's grave wearing a historical costume but . . . did he look a little different now? Jojo couldn't be sure.

"Excuse me, Mister . . . ?"

"Walker," the man said, "Jethro Walker."

Boy, he sure stays in character, Jojo thought, but she said only: "Could you point us toward the next site on the tour?"

"I would be happy to oblige," the man said. He glanced once more at the grave beside Walker's. "Did you know my first two wives are buried here? One atop the other, like they used to do in the old country," he asked.

"Ummm . . . yeah. We heard," Jojo said. It wasn't a detail she wanted in Pip's imagination. She clutched her little sister's hand more tightly and hoped she wasn't paying attention.

The actor didn't let up. "I just want to know who murdered me," he said. "I never saw who fired the shot. If it was my boy, Jimmy, I need to know the reason. Why did he do it? I was a good father to him, although he always was a troublemaker. I *need* to know!"

"Umm, we just want to catch up with our group," Jojo said. "Or any group."

The actor stared at Jojo. For a moment, Jojo felt fear deep in her stomach, like a bear had gripped her innards with its claws. *Probably just the dark and the cemetery*, she thought. But Pip must have felt it, too; she'd begun to tremble.

"That way," he said, pointing toward a memorial on the grave of a little boy with its head missing.

Jojo let out a relieved breath as she and Pip turned their heads and saw a small group standing by the boy's grave.

"Thank you," she said, turning back toward the actor. He wasn't there. Apparently, he'd walked away, although she wondered: *How had he gone so quickly*? "That was rude," Jojo said quietly. To Pip, she said, "Come on. Let's find the others."

As they began to walk away from Jethro Walker's memorial, they heard laughter and turned back. The actor who had initially been portraying Jethro Walker was strolling toward them in his Adidas, leading another group. He had a Coke in his hand from the refreshment tent, which was too far away for him to be the same man the girls had just left at Walker's grave.

Pip came to the realization at the same time as Jojo and began to shake. "Who was that other man we just talked to?" she asked, her voice quaking.

"Just a backup actor, maybe? Like, if someone needs a break?" Jojo said to calm Pip, but she didn't sound as if she believed it herself.

"Yeah, just a backup actor," Pip repeated, nodding her head as if that would make it so.

"Let's go," Jojo said, pulling her sister toward the group ahead of them. When they arrived at the grave of Charles Stodgill Miles, Jojo asked the child actor, "How many actors are there for each site?"

The young actor playing Charlie Miles looked at her curiously, "Just one. Why?"

"No reason," Jojo managed to respond. "C'mon, Pip, let's go home."

Pip was more than ready, and the girls practically ran toward the main gate, the lantern banging at Jojo's legs.

They stopped just inside the gate, breathing hard, to return the lantern. Once outside on the sidewalk, Pip asked again, "So . . . who was that man we talked to?"

Jojo was silent for a moment. "Maybe a substitute actor no one knew about," she said, finally.

"Yeah. Maybe," Pip said quietly, then added: "Can I sleep in your bed with you tonight?"

LEGEND 9

Eyes of the Old Mill Witch

"**N**ot all ghosts, haints, supernatural entities, whatever you want to call them, are scary," Zane said.

"Sure, they are," Ben argued. "By their very nature, they're creepy. I mean, *supernatural* means *unnatural,* as in *not natural.*"

"But some are unnaturally *good,*" Zane countered.

"What?" Ben barked a laugh. "Anyway, that's still scary. Think about it: Even if it was the ghost of your sweet and cuddly great-aunt Erma, you don't really want her hanging around your house. Right? I mean, she'd make things very awkward at the dinner table."

Zane shrugged. The friends were forced outside that day by their parents, who said no more video games (mostly Ben) and horror movies (mostly Zane) until they got some sun on their vampire skin. "Besides," Zane's mom had said before she left for work, "you need to learn there's more to the world than zombies and demons."

So Zane arrived on his skateboard that morning at Ben's back door at the neighboring house. They'd been friends since they were babies, thanks to their proximity.

"Grab your bike," Zane said. "I've got somewhere we can go."

Ben laughed. "My bike hasn't worked since last summer, remember? The chain broke at the end of seventh grade and Dad said I didn't get out in the fresh air enough to mess with repairs."

"Oh yeah," Zane said. "Guess we'll have to walk."

"Wait," Ben said, ducking back into his house. He came back outside with his little sister's electric scooter. "I'll use this."

"Pet will be plenty pissed off," Zane said, using their nickname for Ben's sister, Petunia.

"She'll never know," Ben said. "Let's go. I want to get back to *Call of Duty*."

He hopped on the scooter. When Zane caught up, Ben asked where they were headed, which led to the discussion of "good" spirits.

"Why does it matter anyway?" Ben asked.

"Because we're going to see one," Zane said.

"One what?"

"A good spirit. A witch," Zane said.

Ben nearly fell off the scooter. Zane abruptly stopped his skateboard.

"Are you crazy? Never mind . . . of course you are," Ben said. "The better question is, where do you suppose we're going to find a witch, much less a 'good' one, in Jacksonville?"

That's when Zane explained his plan. They would go to the old cotton yarn mill, which had been vacant since its closure in 2001. Inside, they'd look for the infamous Old Mill Witch.

The boys continued riding in silence until they reached the red brick building sitting still and silent behind its foreboding chain-link fence. These days, the purpose of the fence was to keep curiosity seekers like Zane and Ben away from the building, which was a safety hazard. Back in the early days, management's goal was to keep people *inside* the mill—men, women, and children—working through sickness and through tragedy.

The boys stopped and leaned their respective methods of transportation on the fence.

"It doesn't look very big," Ben said.

"This is the only part of it that's left," Zane said. "There used to be four big buildings. It was built around 1902, so it operated for right at one hundred years. You know how the local history nuts are. They keep fighting to save this building and the whole mill village—all those little houses out on the street. Those were built in the early 1900s for workers to live with their families. Those have been preserved but the city can't find a good use for this old mill building. Every so many years, they say they're going to rip it down. The last time was, like, six months ago, so I have no idea how long it has left. That's why we're here today."

"Do you actually watch the news or something?" Ben asked, looking perplexed at the amount of municipal knowledge his friend had just spouted.

"Nah," Zane said, "but I read the newspaper's headlines on my phone. Ever since the pandemic, I like to keep up with the world around me. You should try it."

"It apparently only leads to unnecessary tours of creepy old buildings," Ben said.

Zane sighed. "You don't get it. We're looking for the Old Mill Witch."

Zane walked his friend to the other side of the building, near the row of houses. "See?" he said, pointing to a historical marker. "That's the story of the witch."

Ben read the embossed wording on the sign:

**Old Mill Witch
Amber-Eyed, Silver-Haired
Ghost of Healer
Who Protected Millworkers
With Remedies and Charms
Still Walks Village Streets.**

"Wow! Charms?" Ben said. "Like voodoo?"

"Not like voodoo," Zane replied, the derisive scoff heavy in his voice. "This isn't New Orleans."

"New Orleans didn't invent voodoo, doofus," Ben said, giving his friend a playful shove. "Anyway, she sounds like she was some kind of doctor. A good person."

"That's what I'm trying to tell you. I looked this legend up online. Here's how the story goes . . ."

Zane explained to his friend how an older woman in the village, likely of Native American descent, was supposedly first seen at the mill in the days of the early 1900s when its employees worked for pennies a day and there were few safety regulations. The bosses were more concerned with the plant's output and profit than with safety and, in some cases, they meted out harsh punishments for poor output. Workers toiled in the incredibly loud mill, feeding their fingers around—and sometimes into—tiny machines. When they were injured, they had to bandage themselves as best they could and get back to work, or they would lose their positions to others who were eagerly waiting for a job. There was no such thing as sick leave. Even if they weren't injured on the job, many of the workers later got sick and died from what was known as "brown lung," an illness brought on by inhaling cotton fibers in the air.

At the height of the mill's unsafe and harsh conditions came the legend of the woman known as the Old Mill Witch. People claimed she was a living, breathing being once, although no records were ever discovered giving her a name or birth date. Now she is known only as a spirit. She's been described by those who'd seen her as having a lined face framed by wild, silver hair. Amber eyes—like a cat's—glowed from beneath her mane. The Old Mill Witch used spells, folk medicines, and balms to help cure workers of diseases and injuries. Her mission was to heal what ailed mill workers because they were required to see a doctor paid by the mill company, who may or may not have the best interests of the workers in mind. She was also thought to be a protector.

"Supposedly," Zane said. "The old witch could commune with ancient Native spirits, and she could perform magic—when any of the mischievous boys in the village stared at her too long, she would temporarily turn them into a beetle or kudzu bug. Another part of the legend said that she cursed the worst mill manager, hastening his death."

Even after the mill closed in 2001, rumors of the witch persisted. People said her spirit was still in the mill, looking for those who needed her help.

People who entered the abandoned buildings claimed to hear footsteps or whispers when no one else was around.

Ben shivered. "You want to go in that dirty old place? The one behind the fence with the barbed wire on top and the padlock on the gate?"

The red-brick exterior was actually in relatively good shape with the exception of some vines growing beneath the eaves. With its rows of tall, narrow arched windows, it looked a bit like an abandoned school.

"Where's your sense of adventure, momma's boy?" Zane asked. "Don't you ever break the rules?"

"There's no way to get over that fence without cutting ourselves to pieces," Ben said.

"This isn't a Scooby-Doo mystery," Zane said with a laugh. "I have a key."

"Where'd you get that?" Ben asked.

"Mom volunteers with the mill's historical society and has all kinds of dusty things around. Let's just say I *borrowed* it."

Once inside, the boys had to wait for their eyes to adjust to the gloom. Coming in from the summer sun to a dim room whose windows were covered in dust and cobwebs made it difficult to see. Some of the windowpanes were broken and covered with plywood. The first room had been cleared out for one of the many projects discussed for the building.

Zane turned on his phone's flashlight. "Let's go upstairs," he whispered.

Ben nodded, then said, "Why are we whispering?"

"I have no idea," Zane said in a louder tone, laughing at himself.

The boys began to climb to the second floor. There, they saw some old equipment that hadn't been sold yet because it was bolted to the floor.

"Can you imagine working here?" Ben said in his normal tone. "It's so depressing."

"Yeah," Zane said. "Kids younger than us worked here back in the early days. Like ten, eleven, twelve years old."

"No way," Ben said. "Wow."

"Yeah, and they weren't working for participation trophies either," Zane said. "They needed the money to help their families survive."

"And the cotton made them sick?" Ben asked.

"A lot of them, yeah. When the workers inhaled the dust, they called it 'eatin' cotton.'"

Suddenly, Ben stopped short and whispered, "Did you hear that? Sounds like footsteps on the stairs . . ."

Zane waited, breath held. "Yeah," he said, also whispering. "Weird."

Ben was about to say he thought he heard soft whispering from above them when he saw movement. "*Ummmmm* . . . who's that?" he asked, nodding toward a dark corner.

"Who's who?" Zane asked, puzzled. "I don't see anyone."

"There. Behind that old machine in the corner," Ben said. "There's a little boy . . . about Pet's age. Except he's wearing one of those caps like in *Newsies*. And weird pants."

Zane squinted. "Hey, I see him now." He was about to walk over to the kid and ask how he got in when he saw a man in an old-fashioned suit materialize in front of the machine. One second, he wasn't there, and then *boom*! Instant man!

"Holy buttered biscuits!" Ben said in a panicked whisper. He'd also seen the man. "Where did he come from?"

The man must have heard them because he looked across at Ben and Zane. That's when they noticed: The man had solid white eyes. There were no irises, no pupils.

"What the . . . ?" Zane said, no longer bothering to whisper.

The boys stood immobile, as if the concrete floor had actually captured their feet. The man turned his watery, white gaze back to the figure of the young boy, who had begun to tremble. The larger figure lifted his threatening hand, holding what appeared to be a giant wooden ruler.

The boy looked at Ben and Zane, eyes pleading for help, just as the man brought the ruler down on the boy's back. The ruler seemed to move right through the figure of the boy, but the boy flinched as if he'd been struck. His wail seemed impossibly loud for such a small boy. The sound went on and on.

"Hey!" Zane yelled. "Leave him alone!" Some part of him knew the boy and the man were no longer living—that they were *ghosts*—but he couldn't just look in that boy's eyes and do nothing.

At the sound of Zane's shout, White Eyes turned his freakish gaze toward Ben and Zane and took a step in their direction. Before he could take a second step, the sound of dozens of other voices joined in the boy's wail. They seemed to come from above them, in the rafters.

Zane looked up toward the ceiling and, without saying a word, gently tapped Ben's arm with the back of his hand to get his attention. Ben had been carefully watching White Eyes but when he felt Zane's tap, his gaze rose and his mouth dropped open. Above them, floating at the ceiling of the building, were spirits of all shapes and sizes, dressed in all kinds of period clothing, their mouths dropped open into impossibly large Os as their wails increased. One little girl wore dirty tights beneath her shabby dress. A teen boy sported slicked-back hair and a white T-shirt. An elderly man wore a work shirt with rolled up sleeves and a pen in the pocket.

Ben and Zane covered their ears but continued to watch the scene unfold. White Eyes seemed unfazed by the haunting chorus and looked as if he might hit the boy again when, suddenly, the sound of a woman's rumbling laughter filled the room. It sounded like gravel and sandpaper.

"Is it . . . the witch?" Zane said.

"I can't look," Ben responded.

The wails came to an abrupt halt as the woman—the witch?— raised a screech of her own. The boys' eyes were drawn upward. There, in the corner of the ceiling rafters were two gold-colored glowing eyes staring from beneath long silver hair that floated around her head as if she were underwater.

Zane froze, unable to move. Ben screamed, a high, screeching cry. "Don't look at her!" Zane said.

"Don't worry," Ben cried. "My eyes are closed!"

Instead, they looked toward the white-eyed man, who grimaced, covered his ears, and began to bend, as if he'd been struck in the stomach. He bent lower and lower and grew more and more translucent until, finally, he faded away.

Then the room was completely silent. There was no sign of the boy or the white-eyed man or the witch or anything other than a few spiders.

Both boys turned, opened their eyes and ran back down the stairs, nearly tripping in the irregular light from the bouncing phone flashlight in Zane's hand.

Once outside the building, they stopped, breathing hard. Zane locked the door. The sun shone brightly, and no one would have believed them had they told anyone what they'd just seen.

"She really *was* a good witch," Ben said.

Zane hadn't stopped trembling, but they both started toward the gate anyway, wanting to get as far from the building as possible.

Zane started to laugh, body limp with relief. "You should've seen you run!" he said.

"You were running, too," Ben pointed out.

"Yeah, well, you did this really *cute* little hop before you started to run. You were scared out of your britches!"

The boys laughed until they had to sit down on the grass beside the fence where they'd left the skateboard and scooter. Finally, they stopped to catch their breath. Their faces grew serious.

"Let's not tell the other guys," Ben said.

"About the running?" Zane asked. "Of course not. But I can't wait to tell them we saw the Old Mill Witch."

"Think they'll believe us?" Ben asked.

"Does it matter?" Zane said reasonably. Ben shook his head and stood to get on his scooter. It didn't matter. Either way, he had a feeling he'd be seeing the Old Mill Witch in his nightmares for a long time to come.

LEGEND 10

Strange Light at Gee's Bend Ferry

Trainor didn't know why he'd agreed to go to Gee's Bend with his cousin, Davon. Trainor didn't like riding on the ferry and Davon knew it. And the ferry, everyone knew, was the only practical way to get to the small spit of land tucked into a curve of the Alabama River. It wasn't that Trainor was afraid of the ferry boat. He wasn't really afraid of water, either—he swam in the river behind his grandmother's house all the time when he was a little kid. He wasn't sure what it was; riding the ferry just made him nervous.

But Davon had promised his mother, Trainor's Aunt Shurl, that he'd pick up a specially made quilt as a gift for her mother's seventieth birthday. As usual, Davon persuaded his cousin to accompany him by teasing him.

"You aren't afraid of a little water, are you?" Davon asked.

Trainor punched his cousin's arm. "I'm not afraid of the *water*," he said, with emphasis. Then in a quiet tone: "The ferry just makes me nervous, is all."

Riding the ferry had made Trainor nervous since he was

quite small. He'd ridden over to Gee's Bend several times in his life—once on a field trip for school and a few times with his mother and grandmother. It was a remote place where only a few hundred people lived, but it was famous for the unique quilts made by a group of female artisans, using techniques they'd learned over more than a century.

The quilts had brought fame to the tiny community, which had started as a plantation of enslaved people and later became a resettlement neighborhood for African American farmers under the New Deal in the 1930s. The people who lived there were largely poor, but they had eventually been able to buy the land they worked and make the community their own.

The reaction to the quilts had come as a surprise to the residents of Gee's Bend and the world. To Trainor, the quilts looked much like the ones his grandmother made—scraps of fabric sewn together into a cozy covering. He could tell the fabrics of the Gee's Bend quilts were brighter and the designs bolder but to a teenaged boy that didn't explain how the quilts had ended up as renowned artworks that were displayed in art museums around the world. He understood, thanks to his field trip, that the quilts and the tourism they brought were now the main economy for the small spot of land known by Black folks as Gee's Bend and by white folks as Boykin, the official name of the community's post office. The quilts had even been featured on stamps issued by the US Post Office.

Now, looking down into the brown water spraying from the tip of the electric ferry boat, Trainor shivered. He turned his face back to look at the landing ahead of them, thinking of the feeling of safety he'd have with the ground beneath his feet once more.

To take his mind off his nerves, Trainor asked Davon, "Do you even know the importance of this ferry?"

"Yeah, I know," Davon said drily. "It's to get people from one side of the river to the other."

"Naw, man," Trainor said, giving his cousin's shoulder a light shove. "I mean historically. Do you know the history of this boat?"

Davon was accustomed to his brainiac cousin telling him about this landmark or that historic moment. He sighed. "You know you won't stop bugging me until you tell me, so go ahead," Davon grumbled.

Like Trainor, Davon had ridden the ferry to Gee's Bend before—he went with his mother to attend the annual Airing of the Quilts festival, during which the whole community hangs their new quilts all over town for visitors to view. But Davon wasn't big on history and knew little about the ferry or Gee's Bend. So Trainor told him the story of the ferry.

The only good way to get to Gee's Bend from Camden is by boat or ferry. It has always been that way. In the early years, people used a cable ferry—a sort of wooden raft pulled across the river by ropes—to get to town for their errands. For decades, the ferry was the only practical way for the inhabitants of Gee's Bend to cross the Alabama River. Three sides of the land on which the community rested were surrounded by water. The fourth was so isolated that it took more than an hour to reach the next community by automobile.

But in 1962, authorities stopped ferry service by simply re-moving the cable ferry from the water and pulling it up onto the Camden side of the river. They did so, according to Trainor's sixth-grade teacher Mrs. Luellen, to try to stop the Black popu-lation from getting to town to register to vote. The Civil Rights Movement had supposedly brought voting rights to Alabama's Black residents, but some white folks were determined to make using those rights as difficult as possible. They figured if they removed the ferry, the residents of Gee's Bend couldn't get into town to vote.

What they didn't realize was that after decades of fighting for the right to vote, these residents weren't going to be stopped by a long drive. Every time polls opened over the decades, Gee's Bend residents drove the extra miles and they voted. Still, it was more than thirty years before real efforts to restore the ferry began, and another ten before the ferry was rebuilt and put into service in 2006.

When the new ferry was built, it was groundbreaking: one hundred feet long, forty feet wide, and the first electric-powered passenger ferry in the United States. One of the state representatives who dedicated the ferry that day said, "The reason the ferry closed is about as ugly a reason as you can have. It was a symbolic statement. The opening of the ferry is another statement. That old Black Belt we used to have, the one where some people knew their place, is dead."

"So see?" Trainor said. "This ferry is part of a Civil Rights statement."

"Huh," Davon said disinterestedly. Trainor sometimes got the feeling his cousin didn't understand a lot of the Civil Rights history that surrounded them in their home state of Alabama. "Well, we're here now. Ferry's working fine in modern times."

After the ferry docked, Davon stepped off and headed to the quilters' co-op. Trainor followed.

After picking up the quilt with its bright patches of orange, yellow, and blue, the boys headed back to the ferry and Trainor began to feel his unexplained anxiety again. He looked across the water as dusk began to descend, and he shivered.

Davon, of course, took notice and teased his cousin.

"You are such a chicken," Davon barked a laugh. "What . . . you think we're gonna see a sea serpent come outta there? Or river serpent, I guess. If there even is such a thing."

That's when a memory skidded through Trainor's brain, too quickly for him to catch it. *Serpent,* he thought. Suddenly, he caught the memory by the tail. He was taken back to a time when he was about eight years old and was crossing on the ferry with his older sister, DeLisa, and her friend, Tyra. They were fifteen at the time and liked to give Trainor a hard time . . .

"Have you ever heard of the ghost lights?" Tyra asked him, giving a wink to DeLisa.

"The *what* lights?" Trainor asked.

DeLisa picked up the signal and continued the story. "The ghost lights," she said to her brother. "You had to hear about the ghost lights at school. Every year, a group of us from the high school go down to the bank to look for them."

"You're crazy," Trainor said, sure his sister and her friend were teasing him.

"I'm not kidding," DeLisa said, earnestly. "For years, people have claimed to see a light at the ferry landing, shining up from beneath the river . . . a greenish light. Some witnesses claim the light starts small and grows to cover sixty feet, which is, like, more than ten times as wide as I am tall."

"But where would it come from?" young Trainor asked reasonably.

Tyra told Trainor all the legends: Some people said the light was a ghostly emission from a military plane that crashed near the landing decades ago. Others said a riverboat had overturned there. Still others said the light was the ghost of a person who drowned at the site.

"The only problem is—" DeLisa added, "we've looked it up on the internet and we can't find any information at all on any of those things. So the light is a mystery."

Dusk had begun to fall. Trainor was staring down into the darkening water, looking for the light, when the ferry docked. As he and DeLisa and Tyra exited, Trainor stepped too close to the edge of the ramp that led from the ferry to the landing. DeLisa tried to grab him, but she was too slow, and he lost his footing.

Splash! Trainor's head was suddenly dipped beneath the water. His heart seized in terror. He'd never been a great swimmer, but it was the thought of the ghost light that made his lungs clench. He surfaced quickly, sputtering and thrashing. DeLisa and Tyra looked concerned. "I think he needs help," Tyra said. "C'mon, little dude," DeLisa said. She held out a hand, trying to pull her brother back onto the ramp.

Trainor reached for his sister but dipped back beneath the surface. He was pushing himself back to the surface when he felt something touch his foot. Then, the water around him was suffused in light—a glowing, greenish light.

He jerked his leg, but something seemed to hold it fast. He had taken a deep breath before he was pulled under, but he knew he needed to get his foot free, or he would soon be out of air. He'd never felt such terror. His heart pounded in his ears. He kicked his foot again and, in the murky light, he looked down. That's when he saw it. A creature.

He didn't know what it was. It had scales, like a fish. It had some kind of claw, like an oversized lizard, because that is what gripped his right ankle. He nearly exhaled all his air when fear

overtook him at the sight of the being. He managed to hold it in and kicked again, harder. This time, his foot came loose and he rose to the surface.

"Get me out!" he was screaming as he broke the surface. "Help me, 'Lisa! It's going to get me."

DeLisa and Tyra both reached out a hand to him. Just as he was about to grab Tyra's hand, he felt a tug on his right foot again. He nearly went under the water again but kicked as hard as he could and grabbed onto Tyra and DeLisa, who each took an arm and pulled him to the landing.

He lay there, wet and shaking, as the ferry master approached. "Is he okay?"

"I think so, mister," Tyra said. Trainor could only nod.

"We'll give him a minute then we'll take him home," DeLisa told the man. He nodded and walked away.

DeLisa knelt beside her little brother. "Omigod, I'm so, so sorry that happened, Tray. I know you can't swim that well."

He was still breathing hard but managed to say, "It wasn't that, DeLisa! Something was holding me down."

The girls looked at each other. He must be in shock, DeLisa thought.

Trainor saw the look and knew the girls didn't believe him. "I'm telling you, there is something down there. Didn't you see the ghost light?"

"I saw a greenish light," Tyra said, "but I thought it was just a weird reflection. Isn't there, like, plankton or something that glows?"

"That's in the ocean, Ty," DeLisa said. "C'mon bro, let's get you home."

They looked nervously back at the water, but none of them ever mentioned it again.

Trainor shook himself from the memory. He couldn't believe he'd forgotten the incident.

"What is it?" Davon asked. "You look sick."

"I just remembered why I hate this ferry so much, 'Von" he explained. "When I was little, I saw it. I saw the ghost light. And the thing that lives in it."

Davon laughed. "Ghost light? You've gotta be kidding me, cuz!"

"I'm not messing with you, man," Trainor said.

"Why do you look so scared?" Davon continued. "I mean, you're talking about a light. What kind of haunting is that? No serial killer. No kraken. No ghost. A *light*. Not scary at all."

That's what he thinks, Trainor thought.

"I'm telling you there was something in the light," Trainor said. "Something that tried to pull me under the water. I don't have any idea what it was. A ghost? A serpent? The ghost of a serpent? I don't know what it was, but it was *real*."

Trainor shook his head as if to remove the memory. "That light went almost as far as I could see. And *something* tried to pull me beneath the surface."

Now Davon looked worried. Had his cousin lost his marbles? The ferry was docking. He'd get Trainor back home and let his mother figure it out.

"You don't really believe that stuff, do you?"

Trainor nodded. "Oh yes. I believe."

The ferry lurched as it docked. The boys began to walk to the ramp. Davon handed Trainor the folded quilt and began tugging his other arm, worried that Trainor would fall because he wouldn't stop staring at the water.

That's when Davon, who was focused on Trainor, tripped on the ramp and fell into the water.

Trainor's heart froze. He suddenly saw the greenish light moving toward his cousin, who was thrashing in the shallow water.

Trainor yelled: "Get out of the water! Get out! Hurry!"

Davon got his feet beneath him in the thigh-deep water and looked behind him into the river. His eyes grew round as he saw the large area of light moving toward him. What was it? He didn't wait to find out. He scurried, as much as the water would let him, back onto the ramp.

Trainor helped pull him up. "Hurry!"

Once he was back on the ramp, breathing hard, Davon looked back at the water. The light began to recede. As the boys watched it fade, Davon noticed something beneath the surface. Was it a hand? A claw? A tail?

Davon didn't know. He didn't want to know.

"Let's get out of here," he said, and the boys headed toward home.

The Backstories

Which Parts of the Legends Are Real?

While all the preceding tales are based on legends rooted in real Alabama people and places, parts of the stories are just that: stories. That's how folklore evolves: The history of real people, places, and events is sprinkled with fictional and supernatural elements and kneaded into ever-expanding tales.

Why supernatural? Human beings have always been fascinated with mysteries and the unknown. Tales of ghosts and werewolves and mystical creatures give us a way to make sense of things we can't explain, while at the same time allowing us to experience fear in a safe environment.

So which parts of the preceding legends are true?

Following is a breakdown of which parts are based on history and which story settings you can visit today. I do want to point out that some places listed are private property and that most cemeteries close at sunset. Trespassing is illegal and risky, and it violates an unspoken folklorist/historian code.

Introduction

It's true that the legend of Rawhead and Bloody Bones terrified me as a child. I consulted several sources to research its origins, including Scott Poole's post "Bloody Bones: A History of Southern Scares" on *Deep South* magazine's website; Dave Tabler's post "Why Did Rawhead Scare Kids So?" on the website Appalachian History; and S. E. Schlosser's retelling of the legend on the American Folklore website.

Legend 1: The People Under the Lake

Alabama is home to many beautiful lakes, and, according to the Encyclopedia of Alabama's "Water Resources in Alabama" entry, only one of them (Lake Jackson near Florala) occurs naturally. The others were all created by two powerhouse power companies: Alabama Power Company and the Tennessee Valley Authority.

Alabama Power was founded in 1906 and quickly began building dams on Alabama's rivers from Birmingham southward. The Tennessee Valley Authority, formed in 1933 as part of Franklin D. Roosevelt's New Deal, was designed to bring jobs and prosperity to rural areas of the South. It serves Tennessee and parts of northern Alabama.

When power company officials decide to build a dam across a river or its tributary to flood the areas below it and form a lake, they have numerous responsibilities—including how to move the thousands of people who live, work, and play there. They also have to figure out what to do with cemeteries, churches, stores, homes, and all the other things that make up a town. It's staggering to think about.

Weiss Lake, on which you can boat, fish, and swim today, was created by the Alabama Power Company in the 1960s by flooding more than 30,000 acres in Cherokee County. In his book *A History of Weiss Lake*, author Douglas Scott Wright says fifteen cemeteries were moved to create Weiss Lake. In most cases, the power company got in touch with families of the deceased, got permission to move the bones, and reinterred the remains in a cemetery of the families' choosing. But what about the graves that no longer had markers or those whose occupants were unidentified?

It is truly creepy to consider what once was beneath the surface when you play in these lakes. In most cases, the buildings really were demolished. But legends of the ringing church bell or the eerie, echoing barking of hunting dogs persist. What lies beneath the surface of Weiss Lake? The only way to be sure would be to drain it.

Legend 2: The Dead Children's Playground

Huntsville, Alabama, is known as the Rocket City because it is home to the US Space and Rocket Center and NASA, not to mention the army's Redstone Arsenal. It has grown to be the largest city by population in Alabama, although Birmingham is still larger by metro area. Despite the growth, Huntsville has maintained its small-town feel, with several beautiful historic districts and a quaint downtown free of skyscrapers. In 1819 it was the temporary capital of Alabama.

It is also home to a plethora of fun legends and lore. One of the most popular is the Dead Children's Playground. Every teenager in Huntsville and its surrounding areas has heard of this site, and many have visited it. The playground does, in fact, adjoin Maple Hill Cemetery. It is also surrounded on three sides by the same limestone-rock walls that make up many of the cave systems in the area, making it a spot that lends itself to creepy legends.

The 1918 Spanish flu pandemic was, of course, quite real. It was similar to the coronavirus pandemic of this century but with an even bigger death toll: historians write that more than 50 million people worldwide died from the Spanish flu in 1918 and 1919, more than twice the number of soldiers who died in World War I (which ended the same year the pandemic began).

The signs and examples of masking advice in the story are real and can be found at the Library of Congress and National Archives websites. Many of the details come from recordings of Spanish flu pandemic survivors at the Alabama Department of Archives and History.

The first known cases in Alabama were diagnosed in Madison and Conecuh Counties on September 28, 1918. On October 7, Alabama governor Charles Henderson mandated that all public places be closed statewide to help prevent spread of the disease.

As for the burial ground—yes, Maple Hill Cemetery is one of Alabama's oldest and largest. It was established around 1820 and has more than 80,000 burials. The cemetery has some interesting funereal art, including angel statues, ornate crosses, and large mausoleums, several of which are purported to be haunted. It is a beautiful and peaceful place to take a stroll on a nice afternoon. It closes at sundown. Many Spanish flu victims are likely buried in the cemetery, although most headstones do not state a cause of death. Victims were also buried in the cemetery's Potter's Field, which is where people who could not afford to pay for funerals are interred. Many of them are listed on a large monument placed at the edge of the field. If you look, you will note that many of them died in 1918.

Lastly, the children's rhyme about "Enza" was a real song, but it didn't originate during the 1918 pandemic. It had been around since at least 1894, when a version was transcribed by the Massachusetts Reformatory in Concord:

> There was a little girl, and she had a little bird,
> And she called it by the pretty name of Enza;
> But one day it flew away, but it didn't go to stay,
> For when she raised the window, in-flu-Enza.

That verse was later shortened to the one heard in 1918. It was used to try to get people to close their windows, which was then thought to help protect them from the spread of the disease. (Ironically, medical science now knows that the opposite is true—that good ventilation is better for combatting the spread of communicable viruses like flu and COVID.)

Maple Hill Park, the playground, is located at 1351 McClung Avenue SE in Huntsville. It closes nightly at 11 p.m.

Legend 3: The Wolf Woman of Mobile

Was the Wolf Woman real? I can't make that claim definitively because I've never seen her.

I can assure you, however, that the phone calls to the police were real. The article in the Mobile *Press-Register* newspaper was real. The illustration was probably skewed toward parody, but a newspaper illustrator did, in fact, draw a wolf-type woman based on witness descriptions.

The calls to police began near April 1, 1971, a date that made many people skeptical of the claims. But there were multiple claims over multiple days, which would require a lot of coordinated effort for an April Fool's joke. So what did people see in Mobile in 1971? We may never know for sure.

If you want to get the feel for the legend of the Wolf Woman of Mobile, head downtown and visit some of its most historic haunts, so to speak. It is a beautiful and fascinating city that dates back to its establishment in 1701 as a French colony. It is also where Mardi Gras originated in the US. The Mardi Gras celebrations in Mobile are slightly less rowdy than the better-known celebrations in New Orleans and are definitely worth checking out. Just be sure to always pronounce it correctly: Mo-*beel*.

Legend 4: The Ghost Town of Praco

Although Heath Horton is a fictional visitor to the site in this story, the town of Praco, the mine, and the cemetery were all real.

The cluster of coal silos remains on the property, now covered in kudzu and surrounded by heavy underbrush. The mining disasters listed in the story are also real. Mining was, and is, a risky way to make a living.

There are some interesting similarities between Heath's story and miner lore. Miners did use metal tags (sometimes made of brass or copper) to mark their coal carts and show how much they'd dug that day, although I am not sure if they were used in the Praco mines. They were paid by their output so marking their cart was especially important to their livelihoods.

Visitors to the site can still see the street beds and the old coal silo; however, permission to enter the property must be obtained through Walter Energy before going.

In the 1930s, mining companies (in this case, Prattville Consolidated Company) built towns dotted with modest homes that were rented to miners and their families. The owners also built a commissary—a general store—stocked with goods the townspeople might need, from food to household goods to clothing. The workers were often paid in a type of company currency that was only accepted at the company store, which forced them to spend their wages with the owners. In Praco, the workers called this currency "clackers."

These types of communities, known as company towns, were typically necessary in the early twentieth century when mines were located in isolated areas and fewer people had cars to travel to work. The Praco mine, by that time owned by Alabama By-Products, closed in the 1950s. Retired miners and families were allowed to remain in the homes for more than two decades after the closure until Alabama By-Products sent out eviction notices before Christmas in 1981. Evicting people living on fixed incomes from their homes at Christmas drew the nation's attention and even the *New York Times* wrote about the situation. Due to the response, evictions were postponed until the summer of 1982. It was the last surviving company town in Alabama. After that, many of the homes and the store were torn down.

Do the victims of the mining disasters still roam the cemetery? That's the legend people tell around campfires.

Legend 5: They Saw the Light at the Redmont

The multistory Redmont Hotel was built in 1925 by architect G. Lloyd Preacher. Although it has been closed for several periods of time, it has always served as lodging, so it is considered

Alabama's oldest hotel that has never been operated as any other business but a hotel.

The building was luxurious for its time. Each room had its own bathroom rather than the guests having to share one on each floor, and the hotel boasted ceiling fans and chilled water. Even before Hank Williams Sr.'s infamous stay, the Redmont was the source of stories.

In November 1934 a shoot-out between police and two would-be robbers occurred in the elegant lobby, according to an Associated Press article at the time. One of the men was shot and killed and the other escaped. One police officer, Detective A. C. McGuire, was shot but survived.

In 1947, the hotel was owned by Clifford Stiles. He and his family lived in a penthouse on the top floor. If you look at the panel on the elevator in the lobby, you'll see a button marked PH for "Penthouse." According to the ghost website Haunted Rooms America, Stiles is said to still haunt the upper floor of the hotel. That area is now a bar/lounge.

It is true that Hank Williams Sr. stayed at the hotel the night before he left for a concert and died in his car. Historians and internet sleuths debate which room he stayed in—several sources claim it was on the second floor. Some sources claim he stayed in the penthouse, but that is likely untrue because that suite would have been occupied at the time by the Stiles family.

Visitors to Birmingham can stay in the fully renovated Redmont Hotel today; it was reopened in 2016 by Hilton. I've stayed there—it retains its Art Deco style and the original chandelier in the lobby. The room I stayed in was small but elegant, with lots of preserved historical touches. I didn't see Hank, who famously sang, "I'll Never Get Out of This World Alive," but people say he still hasn't checked out of the hotel.

Legend 6: The Mysterious Last Voyage
of the *Gloria Colita*

The tragic story of the *Gloria Colita* is true, as are the details of her origins. She was built by Reg Mitchell of the Mitchell ship-building family. Reg was said to be a hulking figure of a man—some said as much as seven feet tall. The ship was named for his daughter, Gloria Colita Mitchell (whose married name was Greenwood).

In 1940, the *Gloria Colita* left Mobile, as stated, and was dis-covered abandoned with no one on board. The description of what the Coast Guard found upon boarding the ship comes from newspaper accounts at the time. The phenomenon of discover-ing crewless ships was not a new one; they've occurred since the first ships set to sea. Typically, the lack of any surviving crew is blamed on rogue waves—tidal waves or tsunamis—that strike the vessel and toss everyone overboard to their deaths. The *Mary Celeste* mentioned in the story is one of the most famous cases of a ghost ship whose mystery has never been solved.

When entire vessels disappear along with the passengers and crew, people are left with even fewer clues as to what hap-pened. That's the reason many people blame such losses on the Bermuda Triangle. For centuries, ships gliding through the area and planes flying over have disappeared in the triangle without explanation. The stories of *Flight 19* (actually a group of five mili-tary planes that went into the sea) and the USS *Cyclops* (a navy ship that disappeared in 1918 with 306 passengers and crew aboard) are true. Did supernatural elements lead to their demise? Most scientists believe it was plain old bad luck and circumstances.

In truth, the *Gloria Colita*'s planned trajectory had not in-cluded any travel into the boundaries of the triangle, and it's impossible to know if she ever did enter the area. After the wreckage of the *Gloria Colita* was found, she was returned to port in Mobile by a towboat. She would eventually be scrapped for parts. That doesn't stop some people from seeing the ghostly shape of the elegant schooner on foggy nights in the bay. Perhaps her ghostly crew is still on board, hoping a living soul will discover what happened in February 1940.

The ship's namesake, Gloria Colita Mitchell Greenwood, also came to a tragic end: she was murdered by her gardener on the Caribbean island of Saint Lucia in 2011 when she was 79 years old. Sir James Fitz-Allen Mitchell, Reg's son and Gloria's brother, served as prime minister of Saint Vincent and the Grenadines. He died in 2021.

Legend 7: The Ghost Train of Old Railroad Bed Road

I've lived near Old Railroad Bed Road in Madison, Alabama, for much of my adult life and currently live just two miles from the site of this legend. There has never been a railroad there in my lifetime—hence the "old" in its name. The road does follow the path of a rail line that carried passengers and freight through this area from 1887 until 1929, when it ceased operation. The route began as the Decatur, Chesapeake and New Orleans Railway Company but was later purchased by the Middle Tennessee and Alabama Railway.

The rails were removed in the 1930s. The road is now paved and, in some areas, heavily traveled by automobiles. It runs southward from the Alabama–Tennessee line until it becomes County Line Road, which demarcates the border between Madison and Limestone Counties in northern Alabama.

The community of Dan no longer exists but some of its

buildings are still standing. At the intersection of Old Railroad Bed and Baites Roads, you can see the ruins of a store that likely had a post office in it, as well as other buildings that may have been warehouses to store freight from trains and perhaps a small depot or mill. You can see all the picturesque buildings from the road, but the property is privately owned and the buildings are too dilapidated to enter safely.

If you visit, you can take the short drive southward on Old Railroad Bed until it ends at US Highway 72 and view the scenery along the same route as train passengers once did.

As for the train crash: I can find no record that it occurred. I found the story of the ghost train in a publication called *Old Huntsville Magazine*, which gives no source for the tale. Parts of the story I found there checked out, however: the location of the railroad, the remains of a little town, and the natural water source, Toney Spring, in which victims supposedly drowned. Oh, and one more small piece of "evidence": One day, while in my backyard near the site, my daughter and I heard the lonely *hoo-oo-woot* of a train whistle. At first, we didn't react and then our minds *dinged* at the same time. "There aren't any train tracks near here," my daughter said.

"No," I agreed. "But there used to be."

Did we hear a ghost train that day? We haven't found any other explanation.

Legend 8: Who Killed Jethro Walker?

The pertinent details of this story are true: Jethro Walker was a prominent Alabama businessman who invested in plank roads. He was shot and killed in his Auburn home while reading his Bible with another man, Mr. Dubberly, in 1858. His son James

H. Walker did go to the country of Cuba, where a paper trail of his existence seems to end. Jethro Walker's murder was never solved. He is buried in Pine Hill Cemetery alongside two of his wives, who are interred English-style, one atop the other.

Pine Hill Cemetery does host lantern tours each October (as always, check to be sure this is still the case; event schedules change quickly these days).

Some interesting tangents to this legend: the story of little Charles Stodgill Miles and his headstone is true; many of Auburn University's founders are buried in Pine Hill; and you can visit a plank road replica at Tannehill State Park.

Does his spirit haunt the cemetery? Numerous people claim to have seen his ghost but, to date, I have not.

Pine Hill Cemetery is located at 201 Armstrong Street in Auburn, Alabama. It closes at sunset.

Legend 9: Eyes of the Old Mill Witch

The sign that Ben and Zane find describing the legend of the Old Mill Witch is real; it was erected on C Street by the city of Jacksonville in 2021, in conjunction with the William G. Pomeroy Foundation. It was based on a local legend that was the subject of "A Homespun Ghost Story," a September 2015 *Southern Living* column by Rick Bragg, a Pulitzer Prize-winning author and one of the South's favorite sons. Bragg was born in Piedmont, Alabama, and graduated from Jacksonville State University in the town where this story takes place.

Bragg's article says: "Ghosts peered down from the rafters, people said. When the old mill finally shut down, after shaking the earth of my hometown for a hundred years, workers who stayed on to dismantle its machines said they heard strange things when they walked the vast, echoing rooms. They heard footsteps and an unsettling, whispering sound, as if generations who had worked themselves to death refused to depart just because the rich men closed the doors."

In this case, the Jacksonville mill—which over the years was known as the Ide Cotton Mill, the Profile Mill, and Union Yarn— was obviously real, as was the danger to workers, according to Bragg, who wrote a book about mill workers called *The Most They Ever Had*. Operating mill machinery was hard and dangerous work: workers could lose body parts to the equipment; breathing the air (or "eatin' cotton," as it was sometimes called) caused lung disease; and children often worked long hours alongside adults. Owners provided no employee benefits: if you were sick, or lopped off a finger while working, mill owners expected you to do your work anyway if you didn't want your pay docked. Over time, society began to focus on improving the lives of mill workers: passing laws to make workplaces safer, banning child labor, and offering additional employee benefits such as insurance and sick pay. Though the mill eventually closed and many of the buildings were demolished, the building mentioned in this story is still standing as of this writing.

The legend of the Old Mill Witch was probably meant to bring hope and optimism to people who had little of either. Through this legend, they could believe someone was watching over them—that they weren't abandoned.

Legend 10: Strange Light at Gee's Bend Ferry

This part of Alabama, located in an area known as the Black Belt because of its rich soil, has many fascinating little towns, including Gee's Bend.

In the 1800s, Gee's Bend was the site of a plantation. Following the emancipation of enslaved people, the African Americans who once worked for plantation owners became tenant farmers and founded Gee's Bend on the isolated curve of land, according to Billy Milstead of the Rural SW Alabama website. In the 1930s, the US government's Farm Service Administration turned the land into a resettlement community in an effort to ease effects of the Great Depression and help poor farm families find better lives. "Many of the community members eventually bought the farms from the government in the 1940s," Milstead said. Dozens of resettlement communities were established around the country, including at least eight in Alabama, as part of President Roosevelt's New Deal.

True, too, is the story of the ferry, which began as a cable ferry. It was closed in Camden in 1962 to make it difficult for the Black residents of Gee's Bend to get to Camden to vote.

In 2006, the ferry was finally reinstated. It is still the fastest way to reach Gee's Bend. Today, people from across the world ride it over to the small community to absorb some of its history, meet some very talented people, and look at the quilts.

As for the green light . . . stories about it have been told for decades, long before the Civil Rights movement. Is its source supernatural? Does it emanate from a cryptid (a creature whose existence hasn't been proven)? Or does the reason for the legend stem from our innate fear of deep, murky water? Perhaps you should go and find out. The ferry, which carries people and vehicles, is located at 1001 Earl Hilliard Road, Camden, Alabama. Tickets are required.

Gee's Bend is a fascinating place to visit. You can stop at the Gee's Bend Quilters' Collective at 14570 County Road 29 and browse the beautiful designs. Sometimes you can even watch the quilters as they work.

While in the area, visit the nearby city of Selma and see the historic Edmund Pettus Bridge, site of the Civil Rights march known as Bloody Sunday, as well as historic homes, buildings, and the beautiful Live Oak Cemetery.